Murder on the Professional Development Weekend

by

Rosie Cavendish

Miss Clover Lightfoot Murder Mystery No.2

ISBN: **978-1542763325**

Acknowledgements:
Thanks to Margaret Cusack
for her proofreading and feedback.

Dedication

To all teachers, everywhere.

Part 1

Prelude

1996

It was the first assembly of the new school year and the headteacher, Mr Fish stood to address the whole school. The children were seated on the hall floor, cross-legged in neat rows while their teachers perched on plastic chairs. Mr Fish was wearing an orange robe in the style of the Dalai Lama. 'So,' he said, 'hands up if you went somewhere new over the summer holidays.' He raised his own hand as he said it. 'Can anyone guess where I went?' Some hands were raised and he chose one of the youngest children to suggest an answer.

'Was it the North Pole?' the child asked earnestly.

'Not quite, but it was certainly very chilly,' said Mr Fish.

Watching from the side of the hall, Clover wondered how long it would take the children to guess where Mr Fish had been. Perhaps one of the older children would be able to work it out, otherwise, Clover thought, it might be a very long assembly.

'Did you go to Africa?' asked someone from Year 4. That was quite a sensible suggestion Clover thought. She could certainly imagine Mr Fish's robes being worn in the Serengeti.

'No, not quite,' said Mr Fish, 'I went to an ancient temple in the mountains of Nepal. I went there especially to have a think all about the wonderful things we can do together in the new school year.'

Tom Flint met Clover's eyes from the other side of the hall and she matched his mild smile. She had no doubt he was imagining the same cartoonish adventures as she was: Mr Fish walking along a length of rice paper without tearing it and receiving the blessing of a Zen master; Mr Fish, sitting in a tiny stone cave and opening his eyes to the sound of cymbals; Mr Fish engaging in ferocious martial-art swordplay. Clover giggled silently as she looked at the children's faces.

Mr Fish fed round, wooden prayer beads through his fingers as he beamed at the children. 'Sometimes we need adventures to learn more about ourselves,' he said, and Clover found herself nodding in agreement with this. 'Anyhow, a big part of our next adventure as a whole school will be to welcome our new Deputy Headteacher, Mr Billingham.'

Mr Fish gestured towards the slender, rather twitchy-looking man in a black suit, who smiled with his lips very firmly pressed together. Seized with a sudden inspiration, Mr Fish said, 'Mr Billingham, would you like to tell us all something about yourself?'

'Certainly, Mr Fish,' Mr Billingham said smoothly, 'Good morning children!' he said to the whole hall.

On cue, there was an attempt at a response from the children, 'Good morning Mr...' they tailed off as they replied, their voices merging into an uncertain murmur as they each tried to remember his unfamiliar name.

'I'm Mr Billingham, your new Deputy Headteacher. But before I was a teacher, I did a very different job. What do you think that could have been?' he asked, working hard to engage the children's interest. Clover examined Mr Billingham and wondered what on earth the answer could be.

'Were you a podiatrist?' asked Michael, one of the boys in Ellie's new class. Ellie looked over at Clover and smiled. They both knew Michael's mother was a podiatrist and he tended to assume that the majority of the adult population had, at one time or another, worked in a foot-related area of healthcare.

Mr Billingham stumbled only a little at the suggestion, 'No, I'm afraid I wasn't a podiatrist,' he laughed, 'I wish!' he added, picking out another child to answer.

'Were you a nuclear scientist?' asked Marta, one of the new girls in Clover's class. She was studying Mr Billingham intently as she asked her question, as if scrutinising him for visible signs of scientific understanding.

'Not quite,' said Mr Billingham, 'I was actually something called a management consultant, which is a very special job. It's a lot like being a teacher, but instead of teaching lovely children like you, I was teaching adults who run all kinds of businesses. I would teach them all kinds of special lessons about how to do things much better than before.' He beamed at the teachers around the hall, 'Your headteacher, Mr Fish, heard about all the things I was doing and he thought 'Wouldn't it be wonderful if I could come and teach the teachers at your school something new too?' He smiled. 'I agreed with Mr Fish one hundred percent and I was very excited to be asked along to share my special knowledge with all of your teachers.' Clover could see Ellie's eyes bulge slightly at the self-importance of this. She rose from her seat and slipped behind the piano, gently signalling that the time set aside for assembly was coming to an end.

Mr Billingham seemed slightly taken aback at the lack of reaction to the good news he was presenting and he quickly continued before Mr Fish could take over and finish off the assembly. 'I really want everyone to feel like we're all together in a new adventure this year,' he said holding his arms out wide, 'and that's why I've made a special deal with Swanage House, the company that's running our fantastic Year 6 adventure holiday. And, do you know what they've agreed to?' he asked, like a stage magician building up to the best part of his trick. 'They have agreed to allow all the teachers to go along to their adventure holiday park for a special weekend of extra training and learning together, just at the same time as the Year 6 children are finishing their trip.' Clover exchanged glances with Tom Flint who taught the Year 6 class. He could only offer her a confused shrug, he clearly knew nothing about this.

'The very best part,' Mr Billingham announced with pride, 'is that the teachers will have a special discount price for their visit. So it won't be anything like as expensive as it would normally be for them to have such a life-changing weekend full of exciting training activities.' Ellie played a minor chord on the piano, a chord that somehow contrived to sound perfectly indignant. Mr Billingham looked at her in surprise but she only smiled at him sweetly. Clover couldn't help but laugh.

Mr Fish started a faltering round of applause for Mr Billingham's speech which the children dutifully joined in with. Clover caught Sequoia giving her a gleeful look. Though Sequoia had moved up to Tom Flint's Year 6 class this term, she seemed absolutely delighted at the thought of her beloved Miss Lightfoot joining them for the last few days of the adventure holiday. Clover returned her smile but she didn't feel so sure about what had just been announced.

'Thank you so much, Mr Billingham, I can see all the teachers are very excited about this wonderful news,' said Mr Fish. Try as she might, Clover couldn't detect even the slightest trace of irony in Mr Fish's voice as he said these words and she shook her head involuntarily at the thought of the strange weekend ahead.

Ellie began to play the first joyful bars of Chopin's Minute Waltz on the piano.

'Ah,' said Mr Fish over the music, 'I hear that it's time for our new lessons to begin.' He nodded to the teachers, seemingly blind to the sceptical looks that they were giving him in return. Clover rolled her eyes but she smiled when she looked across at Tom Flint. After their recent adventures, Clover thought that a weekend in the countryside couldn't possibly prevent her from getting on with some proper teaching.

1

In a large, dishevelled classroom, Miss Clover Lightfoot jogged on the spot alongside three of her colleagues and a number of somewhat disgruntled strangers, their feet thundered on the floorboards.

Although she did her best to join in with a show of enthusiasm, this was not the way Clover had been hoping to spend her Friday night. Usually, by this point in the evening, she would have dispensed with her marking and would be contemplating a leisurely bath and a good read, topped off with a steaming mug of creamy hot chocolate.

Instead, she found herself at the Swann Hall outdoor activity centre, a large, converted stately home several hours away from London. Its spacious rooms and extensive grounds had been home to visiting groups of school children and their teachers for many years and that weekend the Hall was the venue for a gathering of teacher training consultants.

Clover glanced around the room as she bounced up and down. A variety of suspiciously sudden illnesses meant that the only other teachers who were attending the event from Clover's school were Mr Simon Fish, the headteacher; Jeremy Billingham, the deputy head and Ellie Robinson, Clover's best friend.

Clover had recognised Gryffin Parr immediately. He appeared frequently on television to comment on educational matters. He was an athletic, middle-aged man and he seemed very comfortable with the physical activity, having discarded his suit jacket, loosened his tie and rolled up his shirt sleeves. His jaw was firmly set, however, and he looked rather sceptical.

The very well presented woman next to him was undoubtedly Mrs Julia Giroux, the chief columnist for *The*

British Educational Supplement. She wasn't really jogging but was flexing her knees and moving her arms in a dignified mime that didn't disturb her wry smile.

Clover also identified Jacqui Scarfe, one of her academic heroines. Her book, *Conversations for Learning,* was a volume Clover had read many times and taken its lessons to heart. Jacqui was dressed in rather astonishing colours and was galloping on the spot with a great deal of energy.

Ellie, Clover's friend, shot Clover a wicked grin and jogged a little harder with exaggerated enthusiasm. She was clearly amused by the whole business. Clover couldn't bring herself to go that far and slowed her pace as everyone started to run out of steam.

The man who was leading the exercise from the front of the room clapped his hands to bring them all to a halt. 'Brilliant, brilliant, fantastic everyone!' he said. 'Thank you for joining in. That's the spirit and it's really woken us all up hasn't it?' Clover couldn't help but notice that he hadn't actually been jogging on the spot himself.

'I'm Neal Skinner,' he said, adjusting his glasses, 'and I'm going to give you just a taste of the power of *Mind-Robics*. It's like aerobics, but for the mind. You've all done so well that I'd like you to give yourselves *a learning hug*.' He crossed his arms over his chest and gave himself a squeeze. 'Like this,' he said. His audience copied him, 'Now, as you hug yourself, concentrate on telling yourself what a fantastic learner you are. Hold on tight for 1... 2... 3... Now let go!' Neal took a deep breath and shook his arms out by his sides.

Gryffin Parr spoke up, 'This is all very well but I presume there's some evidence that this actually benefits children's learning?'

'There most certainly is, Gryff,' answered Neal, 'but I'm afraid the full details of the programme are only available when you buy a licence to use it.' He patted a slim manuscript that rested on the table beside him. 'However, I can tell you that

Mind-Robics is based on the very latest research and it's becoming increasingly well regarded in the United States. I'll give you another demonstration right now. Reach out like this,' he said, extending his right hand out in front of him. 'Now I want you to grasp the idea that *Mind-Robics* is a brilliant new way of learning. Take hold of it firmly, that's it. Now pull it closer and push it all the way into your brain. Just like this.'

Neal acted out grasping something in mid-air and pulling it forward closer to him. His hand slowed as if he were working against some resistance and he pushed with more effort until he'd inserted an invisible *something* into his forehead. His palm met his brow with a slap. 'There, it's in there now. After doing that, I bet nobody in this room will ever forget what *Mind-Robics* is all about, ever again.'

'That *is* amazing!' said Mr Fish with his hand pressed against his forehead. All eyes turned towards him. 'I actually think I will be able to remember that forever.' He looked around at his colleagues, his face radiant with joy. 'We really must write a policy on how we're going to make sure we put this into practice during absolutely every lesson we teach.' Clover and Ellie exchanged wary glances. That was not a decision to make so lightly.

Neal beamed, 'Everyone, all together, reach up high and put that idea on your *shelf of memories*, right up there above your head.' he said stretching upwards and miming placing something on a high invisible shelf. Everyone copied his lead, 'There! Now you know exactly where the idea is when you want to start acting on it, don't you?' Mr Fish nodded vigorously at this. Neal opened his arms, inviting congratulations from his audience, and there was a smattering of applause delivered with varying levels of sincerity in return.

'And…cut! Splendid, splendid!' boomed a voice from the back of the room. A portly man with a shock of blond hair switched off a video camera that made an elaborate fanfare of beeps in acknowledgement. It started to whirr and click as it rewound the large VHS tape inside. 'The wonders of new technology, eh?' he said. Satisfied, he patted the camera on its tripod and made his way to the front of the room.

'I am your host, Lord William Wyatt-Churchill-Swann, Marquis of the Duchy of Bleakly-Burke but you may address me as Lord Swann. I am very proud to welcome you all to Swann Hall Outdoor Centre where we host many visiting school parties every year, giving children an experience of nature and team-building activities.'

'This weekend is an exciting step forward for us. For the first time, alongside our regular activities, we are hosting a gathering of leading educational consultants as well as a group of teachers to discuss exciting new teaching methods. Thank you for that little taster, Neal. I am already anticipating what a life-changing event this will be for you all. Rest assured, it will be captured on video in full colour and stereo sound, ready to spread the word to schools everywhere about the wonderful new techniques our consultants offer.

'Before we meet our second speaker, I would like to invite you to make yourselves a cup of tea and show yourselves to your rooms. There's plenty of space so you can sort that out for yourselves. I myself live in the Lodge so you won't have to worry about getting in my way. Let us convene again in a half hour to hear more about the educational delights the weekend will offer!'

Clover looked towards the single plastic kettle by the grimy sink, wondering how long it would take for the dozen or so people in the room to make themselves a cup of tea. Ellie squeezed her arm, 'Come on, let's find our room. I don't want to end up sharing with someone else and there's something I want to show you.'

Clover followed Ellie out of the classroom and towards the grand staircase. The staircase and wall panelling was painted with dozens of layers of thick emulsion, the top layer of which looked like it had been applied some years earlier. The floors were covered with resilient but unglamorous grey, nylon carpet. Ellie led Clover up the stairs and then quickly along a corridor. 'Where are you going?' asked Clover, hurrying to keep up.

'I came on a visit here with my school when I was in Year 6 and I know exactly the room we want, I just hope nobody's using it already,' said Ellie.

At the end of the upstairs corridor there was a much smaller staircase which led up to a small wooden door. The door was ajar, 'Yes!' hissed Ellie and bounded up the stairs. The room was a square tower room with two narrow beds and four leaded, arched windows, one on each wall. It was decorated in the same sparse style as the hallways but it was a beautifully proportioned space and evening sunlight poured in through one of the windows to illuminate two small bedside tables and a simple desk. 'Oh Ellie, it's beautiful,' said Clover, going over to the window to see the view.

Outside, she could see the grounds of Swann Hall in the setting sun. The surrounding landscape was a sea of emerald green. Clover worked the latch on the window and it creaked open. The Lodge, where Lord Swann himself lived was clearly visible facing the main house across an enormous lawn. Off to one side, Clover could see a set of buildings that looked like stables and beyond them a lake that glittered with the last rays of the setting sun.

In the distance was a group of children and even from the turret room, Clover could recognise her old class from last year. At the front of the group was Tom Flint, their new teacher. Clover bit her lip as she watched him thoughtfully. 'I think it still has the potential to be a lovely weekend after all,' she said to Ellie over her shoulder. 'It might be just the thing to bring the whole school together.'

There had been an unsettled mood in the school following a set of rather extraordinary incidents last term but the summer break had a magical way of resetting the universe and giving everyone a chance at a fresh start. 'As long as we can get through this weekend without anybody being murdered, I think we'll be fine,' said Ellie.

2

'Let's go and say hello to Tom and his class,' suggested Clover. 'We've still got time and I need a breath of air before I'm exposed to any more brilliant new ideas.'

'Put your trainers on and I'll race you,' said Ellie. The two of them were downstairs before Tom and the children had even made their way out of the woods and onto the big lawn.

Swann Hall must have been pretty impressive in its day, thought Clover. The enormous front door and the stairs that led up to it, now augmented by a rickety-looking wheelchair ramp, had been designed to impress the importance of the occupants on anyone who visited. Many years of school journeys had taken its toll, however, and the great house now seemed careworn and impractical.

The children looked excited and full of their usual energy. They were all wearing bright plastic jackets in case the weather turned nasty. The jackets were various shades of vivid neon, making the children stand out against the fresh green grass as if they'd been coloured in with highlighter pens. It wasn't wasn't aesthetically pleasing but it would certainly make it difficult to lose anyone.

Spotting Ellie and Clover, the children bubbled with glee as they broke out of their line to run out to meet them. Ellie feigned an expression of mock horror and pretended she was running away from the approaching swarm of children. The children caught onto the game instantly and ran after her with howls of joy. They might have been hiking for a long time but they never tired of running and playing. Tom Flint, on the other hand, looked like he was feeling the effort. He'd been with the children all week and he was looking very tired.

'How are you doing, Tom?' Clover asked as she approached.

Tom smiled grimly, 'I've been better thanks, Clo.'

Clover narrowed her eyes with concern, 'I'm not sure you look well enough to be going on long hikes. Shouldn't you be resting?'

'I'm fine,' Tom said, shaking his head. He didn't look fine to Clover but he was also the kind of teacher who wouldn't stop if he saw there was something that needed to be done. 'It's just been a long week and I haven't had as much sleep as I'd like.'

'It's difficult to get everyone settled down to sleep on a trip like this, isn't it?' said Clover in agreement. 'Aren't there any other staff around to help you?'

'I was expecting some extra help but apparently there isn't any. I suppose it's just the time of year, residential trips are less popular in the autumn term, so I think we're the only ones here. I don't mind doing it now though, it's a great chance to get to know the children and make a connection, everything's much easier after that.'

'I know,' said Clover, exchanging smiles with Sequoia. The girl had been in her class in the previous year. Clover waved as Sequoia dodged around several of the boys to be the first to catch Ellie. 'You're so good at getting on with them, I bet you already know what makes them tick.'

'There are some interesting characters in there, that's for sure,' said Tom with a smile. 'But if you have any tips for stopping Josh and Jake from turning everything into a running battle then I'd be glad to hear them.' The twins were currently on either side of Ellie, pulling on her hands, each with their own friends in attendance.

'I thought it was best to try to keep them separate so they could find a sense of who they are as individuals without having to compete with each other so much.' Clover said. 'It seemed like a good idea at the time but maybe it's gone too far.' She eyed the two rival groups gathered around each of the boys. 'I'll let you know if I have any new ideas about establishing peace in our time.'

Ellie freed herself and came over. 'Are you ready to go and hear more about the Next Big Thing? There's never just one big thing these days, is there?'

Clover shook her head. 'I think I'm needed here, I'm not sure that Mr Flint should be left to sort out all the children for bedtime on his own tonight, especially if he's not been getting enough sleep. What do you say Tom?'

'Oh, I couldn't ask you to do that!' said Tom.

'Then it's a good thing you don't have to ask me,' said Clover, 'I'm going to stay with you and help out.'

'You really don't look well,' said Ellie looking at Tom. 'Maybe I should come and help you both.'

Clover grinned at her, 'Are you trying to avoid going back inside too?' she asked.

'I wouldn't have to avoid it if it wasn't such a waste of time,' said Ellie. 'I reckon Lord so-and-so spent all his money on getting big name education consultants rather than hiring extra staff to run his activity centre properly.'

'I don't think Lord Swann spends his money on anything at all if he can avoid it,' said Tom. 'This place is a mess. The climbing activities were all cancelled because the equipment is out of date and there were only two ponies available for pony trekking, so we had to draw lots to decide who was going to get a turn. It feels like the whole place is on the brink of getting shut down.'

'All the more reason you shouldn't have to deal with this alone.' said Clover. 'Ellie, could you tell Mr Fish where I've got to?'

'I'll let him know what you're doing and I can update you both on anything that's worth hearing about later on,' said Ellie with a smile and she set off back towards the house.

Clover glanced at Tom and suddenly she felt strangely shy. She never felt this way at work but out in the countryside with the children playing so happily and the fresh evening air all around them, she suddenly felt like she might blush.

Tom frowned and Clover followed his gaze to see what was troubling him. Ellie had stopped to talk to Jeremy Billingham, their Deputy Headteacher, and the two of them seemed to be disagreeing. As Clover and Tom watched, Mr Billingham set off in their direction. Ellie held up her hands helplessly and turned towards the main building.

'Is everything alright here? Should we be calling you an ambulance, Mr Flint?' asked Mr Billingham as he approached.

'Not just yet,' said Tom with a grin, 'I'm just a little under the weather, that's all.'

'Well in that case, I'll need Miss Lightfoot to come back inside and get the benefit of listening to the wonderful consultants we have at our disposal.'

'It was my understanding that our attendance this weekend was an entirely voluntary affair,' said Clover, 'and, after all, we did have to pay our own costs. In my opinion, I'm needed out here and Ellie's going to take notes for me so I don't miss out on anything,' said Clover, not budging.

'I don't think it's entirely fair to ask Miss Robinson to do that for you, Miss Lightfoot. There are some very important people in there, don't you think you'll be letting the school down if you can't be bothered to come and join us?' said Mr Billingham.

Clover considered this, 'No, I don't think anyone else would see it that way. I'm sure all your consultants have been teachers at some point in their careers, so I'm sure they'll understand that it's important to lend a hand to a colleague when it's needed.'

'Well I'm quite happy to tell Mr Fish that you seem to be avoiding an important training opportunity on a whim, if that's the case, Miss Lightfoot.' Clover was stung by this.

‘That’s not the case at all Mr Billingham. Surely you can see that someone should be helping out here right now or are you so focused on appearances that you don’t care about what happens to your own staff?’

Billingham flushed but Tom spoke up gently defusing the situation, ‘You go ahead,’ he said to Clover. ‘I can manage to sort out this lot tonight. Really, it’s OK.’

Clover felt a creeping sense of embarrassment at the whole situation as she wondered if there were any selfishness in her thinking. Maybe it was a fair criticism. She looked at Tom, who definitely looked unwell. Sometimes things were complicated.

‘Alright Tom, but take care of yourself,’ she said, squeezing his shoulder before turning her back on Mr Billingham and setting off towards the house. ‘OK,’ she murmured under her breath, ‘Let’s go and see what fresh wonders these consultants have in store for us now. This had better be good.’

3

Clover felt foolish and a little guilty as she hurried back and went straight into the classroom. Maybe she’d got a bit carried away with the loveliness of the outdoors and now she felt a little ashamed of herself. Ellie had made her a cup of tea and Clover gave her a smile of thanks as she took her seat.

Lord Swann fussed over his video equipment at the back of the room but this didn’t stop him from addressing the assembled group as he ducked down to fiddle with power cables. ‘Greetings again one and all! Welcome back once more. I trust you had a nice little break and a chance to settle in.’ His video camera tootled a fanfare of delight as it accepted a fresh video tape.

'Our next speaker needs no introduction. As one of the leading lights of the teaching profession, he's well accustomed to being in front of television cameras.' Lord Swann turned on the spotlight that was fixed to the side of his own camera and the front of the room was lit up with a glaring beam of brilliance. It was so bright that it looked as if the sun were shining in through the windows, even though it was already evening.

'Please welcome Mr Gryffin Parr,' declared Lord Swann as he aimed the camera. The assembled group applauded with genuine enthusiasm as Gryff rose from his seat and made his way to the front of the room.

'Thank you, thank you,' he mouthed with a self-deprecating smile as he took his place. 'You all know me, don't you?' he began, opening his palms to the audience. His warm, Cornish accent was quite recognisable and for a moment Clover felt glad that she'd been summoned back inside. Gryff's confidence was relaxing and she felt as if she were in safe hands.

'I'd like to introduce you to the idea that's at the heart of my new book. I call it *The Heroic Journey* and I'd like to share it with you now. First of all, I'm going to need some volunteers. Is there someone here who teaches in the infants, or *Key Stage One* as we're supposed to say these days?'

Ellie, Jacquie Scarfe and a third woman, whom Clover didn't recognise, raised their hands. The unknown woman's striking fuchsia-coloured blazer and turquoise silk blouse offset her jet black hair, cut in a stylish bob. Gryff nodded to her immediately and invited her to introduce herself to the room. 'Certainly,' she replied. 'I'm Sophie King and my expertise is in *inspirational* and *aspirational* learning for Key Stage One.'

Gryff nodded, encouraging Sophie to continue. 'My work is about motivation. You may not have heard of me as I'm not published yet but my husband says that's only a matter of time, isn't that right Bernard?' Without being able to take her eyes off Gryff, Sophie gestured towards Bernard King, a much older man with a hairline that had long since receded. He wore a tweed suit and had rather a sour expression on his face.

Gryff grinned, 'Let's make use of you too Bernard, if you'll join me in this little demonstration?' Bernard muttered something by way of a reply and got to his feet.

'I'm sorry, what was that?' Gryff asked.

'I was merely observing that I hadn't actually volunteered,' said Bernard, pointedly.

'Well don't worry, all you have to do is stand there and look unpleasant,' replied Gryff cheekily and Sophie King beamed at him, blushing a little. She was so focused on Gryff that she seemed to have become oblivious to the fact that both the audience and her husband were watching her. Clover rolled her eyes. It was easy to imagine that Gryff might be fairly attractive to many of his audience but the way he was playing with Sophie's interest was quite off-putting.

'Now,' said Gryff, I just need one more person to help me out.' Another hand went up at the back of the room and Gryff beckoned the final volunteer to come and join him at the front, 'What's your name?' he asked as the new person came forward.

'I'm Zuzana Zuleika,' said the young woman, who had a trace of a South African accent. She had straight, cropped hair and was wearing a blue tracksuit. 'Call me Zuzie. My research investigates how contact with animals can help children to learn.' Gryff nodded welcoming her to the front of the room before his eyes strayed back towards Sophie King.

He looked around the room, searching for something. His gaze fastened on a bright yellow folder that was resting on Julie Giroux's table. Gryff stepped forward and picked it up carefully, 'Pardon me Julie but would you mind if I used this folder as a prop? I could have chosen anything but this is such a lovely bright colour.'

Julie Giroux waved magnanimously in agreement as Gryff took the canary yellow folder and passed it to Zuzie. 'If you would be so kind as to hold this, Zuzie, and Bernard, if you stand just here, all will become clear.' Once everyone was positioned to Gryff's satisfaction, he turned towards the camera with a warm smile.

'So, this is what *The Heroic Journey* is all about,' he said as he stepped closer to Sophie King and met her eyes, 'Let's say that we have our precious young learner but at the very beginning she doesn't even know that there's anything to learn. It's as if she were asleep.' Sophie picked up on the idea at once, placing her palms together and closing her eyes, pretending to rest her head.

Gryff looked into the camera, 'Now Sophie, you've been a teacher in the infants. What do you think a Year One child might say if I asked the question: *what's the difference between the number two and the number five*?

Sophie smiled, keeping her eyes closed, 'I would expect a typical Year One child to say something like, *They're different numbers from each other. One of them looks like this,*' she drew a number 2 in the air with her finger, '*and the other one looks like this,*' she drew the figure of a number 5.

'Exactly!' said Gryff with delight. 'So at the beginning of the *Heroic Journey* we need to wake up the child to what they don't know.'

Without warning, Gryff's voice changed, suddenly sounding cold and harsh, 'Sophie, what you're thinking now is completely wrong.' Sophie's eyes snapped open in surprise at his sudden change in tone. 'Of course 2 and 5 are different numbers but I asked you *'What is the difference between them?'* That is a different question.' Sophie looked worried.

'Don't panic!' said Gryff, turning his smile back on as quickly as he'd turned it off. 'I know it's unusual to take such a negative tone but it's all part of my theory. I call this stage of *The Heroic Journey, The Trumpet* because it is a call to adventure. Sometimes we need to give children a little shock to wake them up to what they don't know. That sounds rather horrible, doesn't it?' he asked. Clover found herself nodding her head quite insistently. 'Well, hear me out,' said Gryff. 'Normally we try to teach children without showing them any emotions at all but I believe that putting some feeling into our teaching can help things to make sense. Sophie, how did it feel when I spoke to you like that?'

'Not very nice,' said Sophie, less sure of herself now.

'This is the part of *The Heroic Journey* that I call, *The Cave.* It's dark inside the cave, emotionally speaking, but it gives children the chance to face up to the idea that there are things that they don't know.'

Gryff put his hands on Sophie's shoulders and swivelled her around towards Bernard, 'In the cave there's a horrible monster called *Confusion,*' said Gryff slyly. Bernard shook his head dismissively, he clearly wasn't enjoying playing his part. Sophie looked rather uncomfortable and Clover felt even more uneasy.

'Look over there,' said Gryff, pointing past Bernard to where Zuzie held Julia's yellow file. 'The prize is waiting for you if you can defeat the confusion monster. All you need to do is to steal the prize and escape from the cave.'

'But how?' asked Sophie looking at Gryff helplessly.

'Aha! You need my help!' Gryff spun Sophie around so that they were face to face and squeezed her shoulders. 'I've got a *Magical Weapon* for you Sophie! You can use it to defeat *Confusion* if you do what I say.' Sophie nodded her agreement.

'Good girl. The *Magical Weapon* that we're going to use in this case is a technique called *counting up.* All you have to do to find the *difference* between two numbers is to *count up* from the smallest number until you reach the big one and how many numbers you count is what we call the *difference* between the numbers.'

Gryff turned Sophie around again to face Bernard, 'The *Confusion Monster* wants to know the *difference* between 2 and 5, Sophie. Can you use your *counting up* to defeat him?' asked Gryff urgently.

Sophie nodded, 'I can count up. *3, 4, 5.* The *difference* between 2 and 5 is *three* numbers,' she said rather nervously.

'Victory!' cried Gryff, gloating. 'The *Confusion Monster* is defeated. You can even give him a little slap on the cheek if you like,' he added wickedly. Sophie raised her hand for a moment but dropped it again as Bernard glared at her. 'That part was just a little joke,' said Gryff, 'but I hope you can see the power of *The Heroic Journey.* By daring to add some negative emotions and turning it into a little drama the child can learn a lesson that they won't soon forget. Why don't you claim your prize, Sophie!' Sophie timidly collected the yellow file and all three of the volunteers made their way back to their seats.

'Putting a sense of adventure back into learning is what it's all about,' declared Gryff. 'I'll take any questions but, first of all, thank you very much for listening.' He winked surreptitiously at Sophie as the small audience began to applaud.

Clover turned around and saw that Mr Fish and Mr Billingham had actually got to their feet to give Gryff a standing ovation. So many parts of the performance had made Clover uncomfortable that she found it difficult to imagine how it could be delivered in a classroom setting without upsetting the children.

'Questions?' asked Gryff smoothly.

'My question is, where on earth did you get this insensitive, recycled codswallop from?' said a voice from the front. Jacqui Scarfe was sitting with her arms folded and she seemed to be in a furious huff. 'These theatrics are all very well for a short assembly but to propose this *Heroic Journey* of yours as any kind of serious practice seems inconsiderate, bullying, utterly disrespectful to the rights of the child and potentially damaging to children's education. Not to mention that it seems rather more creative than the usual nonsense you come up with. So, while you're at it, why don't you tell us who you stole this ridiculous nonsense from!'

The spotlight went out as Lord Swann abruptly switched off the video camera but before Gryff had a chance to reply to Jacqui, Neal Skinner raised his hand.

'Why are you being so closed-minded about all this?' Neal asked. He rocked back on his chair and scratched his beard. 'I don't think you should dismiss Gryff's ideas without at least giving them a chance.'

Jacqui Scarfe turned her glare towards Neal, 'I've studied how children learn and if you think that Gryff's little pantomime is full of exciting new ideas then you should go and read a book or two. You could start with Vygotsky and Piaget. They understood that it takes some effort to learn but turning everything into an aggressive psychodrama isn't going to make it any easier.'

Julia Giroux cleared her throat, 'Well despite that, this seems like a very imaginative new approach by Gryff. I think it could really connect with people and raise some interesting questions.'

Jacqui looked around the room, realising she had fewer allies than she'd expected, 'Julia, just because something might become popular, doesn't make it a good idea. Everything we know suggests that children learn best when they're building on what they already understand, adapting their ideas and collaborating with others. What Gryff is describing sounds like a much more violent process.'

Neal disagreed, 'I don't think there's anything wrong with a bit of violence when it's necessary. Lots of kids' stories have a monster or a dragon that has to get killed and it definitely makes things more exciting.'

Jacqui ignored him and appealed to Gryff directly. 'I'm not saying that your ideas have no value at all but this feels like one of those fads that's been repackaged to sell to trainee teachers. Where did you find this one? From a screenwriting manual? Joseph Campbell was writing about this in *Hero with a Thousand Faces* back in the 70s, it's hardly original.'

This seemed to make Gryff absolutely livid and Clover couldn't help but smile. Perhaps Jacqui really had guessed where Gryff got his ideas from. 'Well, for a *fad,* it's selling very well compared to *some* people's work,' sneered Gryff.

Jacquie bristled, 'Just what are you implying?'

Neal smirked, 'He's pointing out that you are suffering from a touch of professional jealousy.'

'I don't see that I've got anything to be jealous about. I don't measure my success by how many times I've been asked onto the evening news. I'm only interested in helping children learn,' said Jacqui.

Neal shook his head, 'Nobody's queuing up to buy your books. Maybe you should pay more attention to what's new and exciting instead of just badmouthing it.'

Bernard King was still rather red in the face from his turn as the monster in Gryff's demonstration but he found his voice again.

'Perhaps Gryff should pay some attention to how his approach makes participants feel before he continues with this line of thinking.'

'Perhaps you should be paying more attention to your wife before you continue with anything,' Neal said, under his breath, giving Sophie King a flirtatious wink.

Clover looked back at Mr Fish and Mr Billingham, neither of whom seemed eager to speak up, 'This isn't any way to treat each other,' she said, blushing. 'Jacqui's made an important point. We shouldn't be ignoring decades of research. We have to consider what's best for the children and put that first.'

'This is exactly why our whole profession is so stuck in the mud,' said Neal, shaking his head. 'You're all far too focused on playing it safe. That's what makes my own manuscript so important.'

Lord Swann launched into a violent coughing fit at the back of the room. Neal ignored him and continued, 'All I'm saying is that I agree with Gryff. We should be trying out new ideas and that's why *Mind-Robics* explores alternative approaches to education from ley lines to healing crystals and the power of opening your chakras.'

'Neal, no!' said Zuzie in a warning voice. Everyone looked around at her in surprise. Clover wondered how familiar Zuzie was with Neal's work; they hadn't been behaving as if they knew each other at all.

The room was quiet for a minute until Jacqui Scarfe broke the silence, 'So that's what's in Neal's precious manuscript: superstitions; lucky charms; and circumstantial evidence. You must be joking! Haven't you got any regard for the facts at all? You're intending to sell that to schools and take their money? How can you live with yourself?'

She rounded on Gryff, 'You're just as bad as him, you know. You're parasites, peddling nonsense, packaged as research. If you're looking for a monster in this scenario, you should go and take a good, long look in the nearest mirror!'

4

'Before anyone says anything they regret, I suggest we all get a good night's sleep,' said Lord Swann, soothingly. 'Some of you have had long journeys here and the filming will be even better if we do it during daylight hours.' A few hard looks were thrown in his direction. The quality of light for Lord Swann's film project was the last thing on anyone's mind.

'I'm sure you'll find your rooms very comfortable and we'll meet again for breakfast tomorrow morning when I hope we'll all be in better spirits. With that, I bid you all goodnight!'

Gryff and Sophie King left the room together with Bernard King following close behind them. Neal and Zuzie were whispering angrily in the corner of the room while Julie Giroux sat at her desk, eyeing them curiously. Mr Fish and Jeremy Billingham seemed to be the only people in the who looked happy. Lord Swann was playing back his recording of Gryff's talk and watching through the eyepiece of his video camera, headphones pressed to his ears as he squinted with concentration.

Clover gave Jacquie Scarfe a shy smile. 'I really admire your work,' Clover said.

Jacqui relaxed, 'You might be the only one,' she said with a sigh, packing up her things. 'I'm afraid it might be a bit too cerebral for this modern age.'

'I don't think so at all,' said Clover. 'Your ideas about the power of conversations and dialogic learning made all the difference to me as a young teacher.'

'Me too,' added Ellie.

'I do think a real conversation, where you actually connect with a fellow human being can be enormously important,' said Jacqui. 'I'll try and explain more when it's my turn to give a presentation but somehow I don't think my audience will be very receptive.'

'*Some* of your audience will be,' said Clover firmly. 'Personally, I can't wait.'

As they left the classroom, Clover noticed that the opposite wing of the house was already in darkness and the dormitory doors were closed. Time had flown by and Tom must have got the children off to sleep already. Clover followed Ellie up the grand stairs to the top corridor, feeling a deep sense of tiredness. It seemed as if her day of teaching back at school and the evening's events were two completely different days that had somehow been crammed into one. She could barely keep her eyes open as she took her things down to the bathroom to brush her teeth.

Padding up the small flight of stairs in her slippers she found that the tower room looked very different from how she'd left it at sunset. Ellie had turned the main lights off and the only illumination came from a torch lying on the bedside table, making the room feel small and cosy.

Ellie was nowhere to be seen and Clover looked around for her for a moment in confusion. Then she heard a giggle coming from outside the half-opened window. 'Ellie?' she asked. This just elicited another giggle. Clover approached the window and looked outside.

Ellie was sitting outside the window on an iron fire-escape. She was only wearing her pyjamas but the autumn air was pleasantly cool rather than chilly. Ellie had taken a pillow to sit on and she was dangling her legs through gaps in the railings, peering out over the deep darkness of the countryside.

'When I came here as a child I sneaked out here every night after everyone had fallen asleep, said Ellie dreamily. It's just exactly as I remember it.' Clover climbed delicately through the window and sat down beside Ellie on the other half of the pillow. 'I was in the juniors at the time,' said Ellie, 'we still called it the juniors back then, not Year 4. Sneaking out here was the first time I ever broke a rule and got away with it without anything bad happening.'

Clover sat quietly, listening to the sounds of the trees and night air, 'I don't blame you,' she said. 'It's really beautiful out here.'

They both fell silent as they heard a door creaking open far below. The door clicked shut and they heard the sound of footsteps on gravel as someone left the main house and followed a path around the side of the building.

'Probably just Lord Swann heading back to his Lodge,' whispered Ellie. 'I bet he's got every luxury under the sun over there.'

The door creaked open for a second time but this time no footsteps could be heard. Clover guessed that someone was walking on the grass rather than the path. She looked questioningly at Ellie who shrugged.

‘Maybe it’s the ghost of Hatton Hoo,’ said Ellie.

‘The what?’

‘I’m sure they don’t mention it any more but when we came here they told us about a ghost who roamed around the house at night. It was the spirit of an ancient king buried under Hatton Hoo.’

‘Hatton Hoo? I didn’t even know that was near here,’ said Clover.

‘Oh it’s really close, you can actually see it from up here during the daytime, not that there’s anything to see, it just looks like an ordinary hill. Nobody even knew it was an Anglo Saxon burial mound until the sixties: they just thought it was an ancient hill fort. I’m not surprised they’ve stopped telling the ghost story though, it was pretty terrifying.’

‘Well now you have to tell me,’ said Clover, poking Ellie with her elbow.

‘There’s nothing to tell,’ laughed Ellie, ‘it was just a creepy story of a ghostly warrior who’d drag people off to live with him under the hill in his barrow. In reality it was probably just another way of scaring children into staying in their rooms after lights out.’

‘It didn’t keep you off the fire escape, though.’

‘No, it didn’t.’ Ellie agreed.

A peaceful silence prevailed for a few moments.

‘I’m worried about Tom. He really didn’t look that well,’ said Clover eventually.

‘Maybe you should go and see how he’s doing now?’ said Ellie. Clover couldn’t see her face but she could hear that Ellie was smiling wickedly at the suggestion.

‘What?’ asked Clover, ‘I’m just worried about him.’

‘Oh yes, of course, you probably should go and make sure he’s recovered,’ said Ellie with exaggerated innocence. ‘Don’t worry. I won’t tell anyone. What happened with you two anyway? Didn’t you go out to dinner that one time?’

Clover was glad that Ellie couldn't see how much she blushed at this, 'Yes, we did and it was perfectly nice.'

'*Nice*?'

'We just ended up talking about school and teaching all the time. To be honest I didn't feel like we were connecting at all.'

'Well, who's fault is that?'

'Hey! It's not all my fault,' protested Clover. 'He's so shy. I spend time with him whenever I can. I don't think he's interested in me and things get awkward really quickly.'

'Yeah, I always feel paralysing awkwardness when I'm around someone I'm *not* interested in,' said Ellie sarcastically. 'You really should go and knock on his door just to say hello. Tell him you're afraid of the ghost and you need him to protect you.'

'You're outrageous,' said Clover but she couldn't help giggling. 'I'm not doing that.' She was thoughtful for a moment. 'Well, not tonight anyway.'

'We have the whole weekend ahead of us,' said Ellie. 'Who knows what tomorrow will bring?'

Part 2

5

Early the next morning, Clover blinked awake as the bright autumn sunlight drew a shining line of brilliance across the ceiling.

She had just had the most beautiful dream in which Swann Hall was restored to its former glory as an elegant stately home with fires in every hearth and opulent carvings decorating the grand oak staircase. Clover could clearly remember the end of the dream, running out of the house into the sunlit gardens where magnificent flower beds and clipped hedges surrounded a huge fountain. Standing behind the fountain, someone was waiting for her and she started to run towards him. Just as he began to turn towards her, she had woken up.

As the dream faded, Clover surveyed the rather plain turret room she shared with Ellie, who was still fast asleep. The creak of footsteps climbing the small flight of stairs to her door prompted Clover to sit up hastily. She wondered for a second if it could be Tom sneaking up to say hello. There was a firm knock on the door and Clover called out, 'Who is it?'

The door didn't open but there was an uncomfortable cough outside and a voice replied, 'No need to be alarmed, Miss, but we're asking all of the visitors to gather in the dining hall as quickly as possible.'

'What's going on?' Clover called out but the only reply was the sound of footsteps hurrying back down the stairs.

The dining hall was in the opposite wing of the house from the classroom but it was just as large and had the additional benefit of a handsome set of French windows that opened out onto the lawn.

Breakfast was being set out by a rather scruffy-looking man wearing an apron. He was replenishing large bowls of cereal and jugs of cold milk and his dark hair was rather comically restrained by a blue hairnet. Clover and Ellie joined the queue for breakfast and collected a bowl of cereal each. Neither of them had been successful in locating any tea or coffee and the loaves of sliced bread in their cellophane wrappers didn't look particularly appealing.

Lord Swann looked even more unkempt than he had the previous evening. He was talking fretfully to a large man in a suit with close-cropped hair.

'What's going on?' Ellie asked Clover. Clover shrugged.

Gryff had somehow managed to get hold of a mug of coffee and was talking quietly with Julie Giroux. Sophie and Bernard King were sitting at a small table for two but they were managing not to look at each other as they grimly tackled their bowls of cereal. Mr Fish and Mr Billingham looked far more comfortable together, sitting side by side, and both were absorbed by the contents of Mr Billingham's notebook. Jacqui Scarfe, meanwhile, was chatting with Zuzie Zuleika by the French windows.

A youthful, uniformed policeman approached from outside the French windows and quietly let himself in. He approached the large man with the cropped hair and whispered something to him. The whole room seemed to hold its breath.

'Good morning everyone,' said the man. 'I'm sorry that we are meeting under such unusual circumstances. My name is Detective Inspector Bob Marsh and this is Constable Gregory. I'm sorry to have to inform you that one of your colleagues, Mr Neal Skinner, has died. It seems that at some point during the night he let himself into a small storeroom on the far side of the lake where he was struck on the head by something heavy, we believe it was a crate of clipboards, dealing him a fatal blow.'

There were a few moments of utter incomprehension as the words that had been spoken seemed completely meaningless. Clover felt numb and her perspective of the room seemed to shift. The bright sunlight outside began to look harsh and the other people in the room seemed very frail and fragile creatures.

'What?' asked Gryff, the first to find his voice. 'What on earth was he doing out there in the middle of the night?'

'Could he have been looking for resources to deliver his next session?' suggested Zuzie. 'He mentioned to me that he was nervous about that after the arguments last night.'

'Surely he could have waited until morning?' Bernard King said, sceptically.

Sophie King huddled against him, 'The poor man,' she said, bleakly.

Ellie looked horrified. She found her way to a seat and sat down carefully to steady herself. 'We heard a couple of people leaving the house in the middle of the night,' she said, 'one of them must have been Neal and someone might have been following him.' A few people around the room drew breath at the same time and there were nervous glances.

'Miss Robinson is it?' asked Marsh, Ellie nodded. 'Please don't jump to conclusions but it would be very good if you could jot down some notes to help you remember every detail of what you heard. I'll be taking a full statement from everyone as part of our enquiries.'

'Enquiries?' Clover asked.

'Yes, we are treating the death as suspicious, so we are asking that nobody leaves the premises while we conduct interviews and gather evidence about the exact cause of death.'

'I thought you said that the cause of death was a crate of clipboards falling on his head?' said Julie Giroux.

'Mr Skinner has multiple injuries, so unless the crate fell on his head repeatedly, we'll need to take a little time to understand exactly what happened. He may simply have fallen strangely and hurt his head before the crate fell on him but if he wasn't alone then we'll want to get to the bottom of what happened.'

'There's a whole class of children asleep upstairs,' said Clover.

'We're well aware of that, Miss Lightfoot,' said Marsh. Clover noted that he already seemed to have worked out who she was. 'The children are to be sent home as soon as possible. Your headteacher, Mr Fish has given me the particulars of your situation and I'm asking him to make arrangements for the children to return home early. It seems that their usual teacher has been taken ill so Mr Fish tells me he may be asking for your help in this matter.'

'Has something happened to Tom? I told you he wasn't well.' Clover couldn't stop herself from looking daggers at Mr Billingham.

'He'll be fine, Miss Lightfoot,' said Mr Billingham, 'It appears to be a simple case of the flu.' Clover started off towards the door. She wanted to see Tom for herself. 'Just a moment, Miss Lightfoot,' said Mr Billingham, 'I'm afraid I must insist that you keep your distance from young Mr Flint just at the moment. We very much need someone to take charge of the children until they can be collected by their parents and we can't have you getting sick too.'

'I can take over the class instead,' offered Ellie.

'I'm happy for you to lend a hand, Miss Robinson, but I'm afraid I must insist that Miss Lightfoot take charge,' said Mr Billingham. 'As I understand it, she knows the children best and has much more experience with this age group.' Clover glared at him but she could see the sense in the decision and she didn't know what else to say.

'If I can be of any assistance, I'd like to help,' said Jacqui Scarfe.

‘Same here,’ said Gryff and there were some murmurs of agreement from the other consultants as they shared a brief moment of solidarity.

‘Thank you, Ms Scarfe,’ said Inspector Marsh, ‘But before you go anywhere else perhaps you could come with me and we will take your statement.’

‘Me? You can’t think I had anything to do with this, do you?’ Heads turned swiftly towards Jackie as everyone recalled the argument she’d had with Neal the night before.

‘We’ve taken a statement from Lord Swann and we’ve spoken to Mr Fish already, you’re simply the next person on my list,’ said Marsh.

‘Look, I’m sure you’ve heard that me and Neal had a heated discussion but if you think I’m capable of doing harm to anyone, then you could not be more mistaken,’ said Jacqui looking indignant at the very thought.

Marsh nodded, ‘It’s just a matter of procedure so I’d urge you not to take it personally. We will be taking detailed statements from everyone. In fact, until we’ve completed our enquiries we’d prefer it if everyone who’s not directly engaged in taking care of the children would remain in their room.’

‘Given the circumstances I’m sure we’ll be happy to comply,’ said Bernard King, looking uncomfortably at his wife.

‘Very well then,’ said Marsh, ‘I’ll be using the classroom area to conduct my interviews. Could you come with me now, Ms Scarfe? Constable Gregory will be stationed in the lobby if there’s anything anyone needs.

Jacqui Scarfe rose to her feet, shaking her head as she followed Inspector Marsh towards the door. Clover leaned across to speak softly to Ellie, ‘Let’s go and wake up the children. We’ll need to keep them away from all of this and I think I know just how to do it.’

‘I’ve seen that look before,’ said Ellie. ‘What have you got in mind, Miss Lightfoot?’

'Nothing, I'm simply planning to take up the kind offers of help from all these very talented teaching consultants. We should definitely ask each of them for their help with the children.'

'And if you happen to casually interrogate them about what happened last night, then that's just a bonus, is it?'

'Well, don't tell me you think that Jacqui Scarfe murdered Neal over a discussion about a teaching method?'

'It doesn't sound very likely,' Ellie admitted.

'No, it doesn't, but I'm not sure Inspector Marsh shares our opinion,' said Clover, 'So, just to make sure that there isn't a miscarriage of justice, I shall be helping him with his enquiries.'

'Whether he likes it or not,' added Ellie.

'Precisely,' said Clover.

6

Ignoring Mr Billingham's instructions Clover went to check on Tom before doing anything else. She knocked on Tom's door and a muffled sound came from inside. She peeked in. Tom was in bed. He looked very pale and his every movement seemed to require a great effort. 'Hey,' said Clover gently.

'Oh hi,' said Tom, trying to sound casual as he opened his eyes.

'Has someone told you about what's happened?'

'Yes, It's horrible news isn't it? I never met the man who died but it's a nasty shock. I had a word with Mr Fish early this morning but then I had to go straight back to bed.'

'I said you didn't look very well,' said Clover, waggling her finger at him. 'I'm not even supposed to be in here. Jeremy Billingham's terrified of me getting sick along with you.'

'He's just scared of having to take over my class, they can be a bit of a handful.'

'Not for me,' Clover smiled. 'What were you planning on doing with them today?'

'We were going to hike up to Swann's Reach and sketch the ruined folly up there,' said Tom. 'I wanted to take the ponies with us so the children who hadn't had a ride yet could take turns.'

'That sounds really nice,' said Clover.

'You'll have to talk to Tony, he's the one who looks after the ponies and serves the meals. He's actually the only member of staff I've seen here all week.'

'I think I know who you mean,' said Clover, remembering the young man with the hairnet in the dining room, 'I'll talk to him, you need to rest.' Clover took hold of his hand and gave it a gentle squeeze.

'I don't think you're supposed to be doing that,' said Tom with a weak smile.

'I'm not supposed to be doing a lot of things,' said Clover. 'But some things do need to be done.' She tucked him in and quietly saw herself out.

Ellie was waiting for her in the corridor, 'Shall we go and wake the children up?' she asked eagerly.

'You're enjoying this way too much,' said Clover.

'I'm not,' whispered Ellie, 'It's all terrible but we do get to go pony trekking, don't we?' Clover nodded and Ellie beamed at her.

'If you don't mind waking the children, I'll go and find Tony and see what the arrangements are for taking the ponies out,' said Clover.

Ellie nodded and turned to go but Clover touched her arm and drew her back.

‘One more thing. When you wake the children, could you also ask Bernard King and Zuzie Zuleika if they could come and help out too?’

‘Of course,’ said Ellie. ‘But why those two?’

‘Bernard looked really furious with Neal when they were arguing over Gryff’s presentation. So I’d definitely like to talk to him.’

‘And Zuzie?’

‘Neal was talking to Zuzie at the end of the meeting. I’m curious to know what they were talking about.’

Ellie nodded seriously, ‘You’re sure you want to get into this?’

‘I’m only going to ask them a few questions,’ said Clover, ‘If I find out anything interesting then I’ll make sure the police know about it. I promise I’ll stop if it seems like I’m getting in the way.’

Clover headed downstairs and made her way back to the dining hall. Tony was the only person left in the large, sunny room. He was putting out fresh supplies of cereal before the children came down to eat. Clover summoned up her friendliest smile as she approached him.

‘Hi, are you Tony?’ she asked. ‘I’m Clover and I work with Tom. Tom’s ill in bed but he said that there was a plan to take the ponies up to the folly on the hill and give the children a chance to do some drawings. Would that still be OK?’

‘Shouldn’t be a problem,’ Tony replied tersely.

‘I’m sorry,’ said Clover, trying to put him more at ease, ‘It must be strange to keep going when something so shocking has happened. We’re not going to tell the children about what’s happened, by the way.’

‘Course, right you are,’ said Tony bleakly.

‘It was probably just a terrible accident,’ probed Clover, watching Tony’s reactions closely. He sniffed and shrugged.

Clover stepped closer, 'unless there's something you know that I don't,' she added.

Tony looked defensive, 'Course there isn't, it was just a shock, like you said. I'll have the ponies ready in an hour, don't you worry.' He paused. 'It's just that the children's drawing books and the pencils are all in the classroom and the police are in there,' he said.

Clover realised that Inspector Marsh was still interviewing Jacqui Scarfe, 'Don't worry,' said Clover. 'I'll see to that. I'm quite curious about what's going on in there anyway.' She left him and went quickly back through the corridors towards the classroom.

'Excuse me, Miss but where are you going?' It was the young police constable who had been standing in the lobby since breakfast.

'Constable Gregory, isn't it?' asked Clover.

'Um, yes Miss,' said Gregory shyly. She recognised his voice as the one she'd heard on the other side of her bedroom door that morning. When he spoke, Gregory seemed much younger than he looked. 'I'm afraid I can't let you go in there while the inspector is conducting an interview,' he said.

'Very well,' said Clover, 'Then perhaps you can help me. I need some art supplies to keep the children occupied. Inspector Marsh said that the care of the children came first. Could you go in there and fetch them for me?'

Gregory looked hesitant, unsure of what to do, 'If you'll just wait there, Miss, I'll see what I can do.'

'By all means,' said Clover mildly, waving him ahead of her. Gregory knocked firmly on the door and let himself in. As the door opened, Clover caught a glimpse of Jacqui Scarfe and Inspector Marsh looking back at her. The door shut but quickly opened again and Constable Gregory beckoned her to come inside.

Clover stepped into the classroom. There was a very uncomfortable silence between Marsh and Jacqui Scarfe. 'I'll just get what I need for the children,' said Clover apologetically. She offered Jacqui a smile but Jacqui didn't return it. She looked far too scared to smile. Clover quickly found the box of art books and added several pots of pencils with sharpeners and erasers. The uncomfortable silence continued as she finished and Marsh watched her suspiciously.

'Sorry and thank you!' said Clover as she headed for the door. The silence only continued to deepen as Marsh watched her leave. Constable Gregory pulled the door closed behind her and she felt both more nervous and more motivated about her plan to investigate further. Marsh was deadly serious and he seemed very focussed on Jacqui Scarfe.

'Thank you for your help, Constable Gregory,' said Clover, still chilled by the silence she'd encountered in the classroom.

'That's alright, Miss. My sister's a teacher, actually,' he said offering a smile.

'Well, you know how it is then, don't you?' said Clover warmly.

'Yes Miss,' said Gregory, 'Frankly, I'd rather have my job than yours. I wouldn't have the patience for it.' Clover considered the intensity of what was happening on the other side of the door and she wondered how much patience Inspector Marsh would have for investigating the crime. It seemed as if he had settled on Jacqui Scarfe as prime suspect already.

'Well, that's kind of you,' said Clover, 'I've certainly found that just a little patience and a little planning can achieve some very interesting results.'

The sound of running and cheerful squealing reached the corridor. The children had woken up and they were beginning to run back and forth along the landing to the bathrooms. Clover went to see what was happening and found Ellie watching over everything as she counted the passing seconds out loud. The children scrambled to get themselves ready.

'It's boys versus girls,' said Sequoia as she skipped past Clover, 'whoever is first will get first chance at a pony ride.'

'Steady,' warned Clover as Sequoia sprinted for the bathroom. 'Well, that's one way of getting everyone out of bed quickly,' she said admiringly to Ellie. 'I think it's going to be a fun morning after all.'

Breakfasted and ready, the children were led out to the lawn in front of Swann Hall. The thickly wooded hills rose up around them. Even though the sky was a vivid, shining blue without a single cloud in sight, the children were well prepared with their neon coloured rainproof jackets.

Bernard King came out to join Ellie and Clover. He was wearing his thick tweed suit and a deerstalker and he carried a heavy walking stick as well as a pack on his back, 'Miss Lightfoot, Miss Robinson,' he called out brightly to them as he approached.

'Mr King,' said Clover warmly. 'Thank you so much for coming to help out this morning. We could do with an extra pair of hands and I confess I'm really curious as to what kind of a session you could offer the children based on your expertise.'

Bernard's eyes twinkled at this, 'Miss Lightfoot, I am a historian but my views on the teaching of the subject may not be quite what you'd expect.'

Clover beamed at him, 'I'll be fascinated to find out more, Mr King. I studied history at uni and I've always wondered if there was more I could do to communicate my enthusiasm about it to my class.'

'Then I hope today will be a treat for us both,' said Bernard. Clover found it hard to believe she'd suspected him of playing any part in the murder. He seemed completely transformed from last night. Clover just hoped that what he had to say was as exciting for the children as it was for him.

Bernard seemed to be regarding the class with a little apprehension as they chased each other across the lawn. 'Well perhaps, if it would be helpful, I could give them a little speaking and listening game to play as we walk. It would be a fine way of demonstrating what my work is about.'

'Yes please,' said Clover. 'Would you like me to settle them down?'

'No need,' said Bernard, confidently. He seemed suffused with a new energy at the prospect of working with the children. He started a quick clapping rhythm and the class quickly followed his lead in repeating it back to him. As they turned towards him with interest, he started jumping comically at the end of each little pattern and the children copied that too. Finally, at the end of a leap, he knelt down on the grass, beaming delightedly the children followed his example.

'Good morning children. My name is Mr King and I am going to teach you a game to help you to practise your history skills. Any volunteers?'

A forest of hands shot up, causing Clover and Ellie to exchange relieved glances. It was becoming clear just how experienced Bernard was as a teacher. He may have looked rather stuffy the night before but now he was with the children, he seemed to have acquired a sense of mischief and his confidence shone through.

'Hold on, hold on,' said Bernard, 'listen to what you will be volunteering for before you all leap in. The game is called, '*Who is the storyteller?* It's quite simple but I need someone who can suggest a story from a fairy tale. It could be Goldilocks and the Three Bears, or Little Red Riding Hood or Cinderella, anything like that. Hands up if you have one in mind.'

He picked out Josh, who had long since figured out that teachers didn't often pick the person who was waving the most frantically. Josh was sitting up very straight and acting out paying great attention. 'You, sir!' said Bernard, as he pointed approvingly at Josh, 'which story do you have in mind?'

'The Three Little Pigs,' said Josh with a wolfish grin.

'Oh, that's a good one. Come up and stand at the front with me and we'll choose someone to be your partner. Who'd like to volunteer for that?' Almost all of the children raised their hands, even Jake, Clover noticed. Clover found herself hoping that Bernard didn't pick Josh's brother to play the game. The boys could be quite competitive with each other and it could often end in tears.

'You there,' said Bernard picking Jake out with a theatrical double take as he noticed how similar the two boys looked. 'Didn't I pick you already?' he asked Jake.

The class giggled at this appreciatively.

'We're twins!' said Jake.

'So much the better,' said Bernard. 'Join me over here and we can begin. But first can I check that you both know what happens in the story.

'There's a wolf,' said Josh.

'And the three pigs all have their own houses made of different things,' said Jake quickly. Between them the boys recited the main elements of the story and Bernard nodded wisely as they went along to the grisly conclusion.

'Very good,' said Bernard. 'So, let's imagine that I am Jake and I take the first turn.' Bernard shuffled sideways so that he was facing Josh. 'I'm going to tell the story as if I was one of the characters in the story.

'This story starts with a wolf who's very hungry so it's perfectly natural for him to be looking for some food, isn't it?' he paused. 'Can you tell who the storyteller is yet?'

Josh nodded, 'It's the wolf,' he said confidently.

'But how do you know?' asked Bernard in mock surprise. 'I didn't say who I was, did I?'

'No you didn't say you were the wolf but you didn't say the wolf was bad,' said Josh. 'Normally they call him the big, bad wolf.'

‘What an excellent answer!’ Bernard responded. ‘Are you sure you’re not a Professor? Oh no, sorry that’s me.’ His joking around wasn’t hilarious but it was so good natured that the children warmed to him.

‘Jake has succeeded in guessing who the storyteller was and now it’s his turn to be the storyteller and Josh has to guess which character is telling the tale. Do you think you can tell a story right in front of everyone, Josh?’

‘I can do it,’ said Josh. ‘There were three pigs and one of them was really clever. He made his house stronger than his two brothers and it turned out to be the safest because it was made of bricks.’

'I think the storyteller is the third pig,’ said Jake, at once. ‘He’s the one who thinks it’s clever to make his house out of bricks.’ Josh nodded his agreement. Clover let out a sigh of relief. The boys seemed to be working together in the game. Bernard was so much better at this than she’d imagined.

‘Let’s try a really difficult one to finish with and I’ll show you how tricky you can make it,’ said Bernard.

‘Once there were three little pigs and they all made different choices, one of them made his house out of straw and that was clever because it was very easy and quick to make, another of them made his house out of sticks, this was a bit more difficult to do but he did it. The last of the pigs made his house out of bricks and that took a really long time to build.’ Bernard paused as both Josh and Jake waved their hands.

The boys stared at each other as they waited to see who would be chosen to answer. Bernard noted this and realised that there was going to be trouble whoever he picked, ‘I bet you’re both right, but I wonder if there’s anyone else in the class who can guess the answer?’ he asked.

Hands shot up and Bernard picked out Lucy, who was usually very quiet, ‘I think that the storyteller is the first pig because he said that building with straw was fast and the other ones were slower.’

‘You’re exactly right,’ said Bernard. ‘Now as we go on our walk, I want you to take turns practising telling fairy stories to your partner and guessing who the storyteller is. If you’re feeling really confident with this then perhaps you can show everyone else when we take a break from walking?’

Bernard glanced up at Clover who nodded enthusiastically at his suggestion. ‘Any questions?’ asked Clover but there were none. ‘Find a partner you’d like to walk with,’ Clover said, ‘then let’s make a double line so you can walk side by side.’

‘That’s a great exercise,’ said Clover to Bernard as the children organised themselves into pairs. ‘They’ll really enjoy making up the stories.’

‘It’s all about teaching them to spot why someone’s story might be biased and thinking critically about why that might be the case,’ said Bernard.

‘So would you move on to teaching them how to identify bias in historical sources?’ Clover asked.

‘Eventually but it’s good to give them a lot of practice first. I find this is more fun than trying to explain “Egocentric bias” with a real life example. Starting with very simple stories helps them to understand the principle without too many distractions.’

‘It’s very clever,’ said Ellie appreciatively. ‘I’m so glad you could help us out today.’

‘I’m only too glad to be of service,’ said Bernard and he doffed his hat rather comically.

Just then, Tony appeared, leading two ponies. ‘The girls were slightly quicker at getting ready this morning,’ announced Ellie, so let’s see which of you is making a good start on their storytelling and I’ll choose two of you to have the first ride of the day.’

7

All thoughts of Bernard's storytelling game were momentarily forgotten as the children stopped in their tracks to watch the approaching ponies. The first and tallest of the two beautiful creatures had a haughty look and a glossy, jet-black coat with a white star on his brow. The second was a miniature golden palomino with a thick, blond mane and soft, gentle eyes.

As the children gasped with delight, Clover saw Zuzie Zuleika jogging towards the group, dressed in a bright red tracksuit. She waved to Clover as she approached but then ran straight past the children to greet the ponies.

'Hello Stubb,' she said warmly. The palomino's ears perked up as Zuzie vigorously scratched his neck. The black pony snorted and nudged Zuzie on the shoulder. 'Oh yes, you too Starbuck,' said Zuzie, giggling, 'You're so jealous, aren't you? But there's plenty of strokes for you both,' she added, patting the second pony firmly on his powerful neck.

'You seem to know the ponies very well,' Clover said cautiously.

'Oh yes, we are very old friends,' replied Zuzie. When I was young, I used to come here every summer. 'You remember me, don't you?' she said to Starbuck, who seemed intent on nuzzling her hair.

'Did your school bring you here every single year?' asked Clover, surprised.

Zuzie shook her head, shyly, 'I used to come and stay here for the summer when boarding school finished. My parents seemed to think it was easier than bringing me back to South Africa. I got to know these two when they were foals.'

'I had no idea you knew this place so well,' said Clover and Zuzie replied with a smile and a shrug.

Starbuck and Stubb were relaxed as the first two children buckled their helmets ready to be helped onto the saddles. Tony was competent but gloomy as he went about his work.

'Better if we follow the rest of you,' said Tony, 'It makes the horses nervous if there are noisy children behind them.'

'Of course,' said Clover. 'Miss Robinson, if you and Mr King could take the lead, I'll stay at the back with Zuzie to help with the ponies.' Ellie followed Clover's lead. She and Bernard King organised the children ready to lead them along the trail.

Zuzie turned her attention to Starbuck, petting the proud little black pony, who shuddered with happiness.

'You're so good with them,' remarked Clover, keen to draw Zuzie out.

'It's simple, just remember to look at their ears,' said Zuzie, as she scratched Starbuck's nose. The taller of the two horses trembled with obvious pleasure and ducked its head, encouraging her scratches. 'If their ears are forward and perky then you know you've got a happy horse but if their ears are flattened back, then be careful. They do that when they're scared or upset. Even if you know them well you could get bitten.'

'That's a really good tip,' said Clover, 'I've had a little experience with horses but I've never heard that one before.' Clover walked beside Zuzie as they set off, checking that the two children in the saddles seemed comfortable as they set off into the woods. The elm and oak trees that surrounded them were richly decked in shades of bronze and gold, while a grove of slender, silver birches had leaves of flaming red. Sea-green waves of ferns lapped at the sides of the well worn track, motionless in the cool air.

'You're lucky to have spent so much time here,' said Clover. 'Was there some reason you always came to this particular place?'

'Well…there is a bit of a family connection,' said Zuzie dismissively. 'Not that I could stay for free or anything. My father still had to send heaps of money to cousin William each time I visited as a *thank you* for having me.'

'*Cousin* William?' asked Clover, 'You're Lord Swann's cousin?'

'He calls me his niece sometimes but technically I'm his first cousin once-removed,' said Zuzie. 'We're not that close, but family is family.'

'It's amazing luck for him that you happen to be an education consultant too,' said Clover.

'Oh, luck doesn't come into it. He knew I was in teaching and he let me know about this gathering, I'm just starting out as a consultant really,' said Zuzie, 'I've only been teaching for a couple of years but I've got some big ideas and I thought this weekend's gathering would help me to get more established. That's why I agreed to help out.'

'Help out?' repeated Clover.

'William couldn't get anyone interested in coming to an event here at all. I think he only signed me up to get the ball rolling and to try to generate some excitement.'

'So did the other consultants get interested after that?' asked Clover.

'To be honest, the others only started to sign up after William asked Neal to come along. Neal had these exciting new ideas from America and once we started to promote them we didn't have any problem finding people to accept the invitation.'

'So that's how you knew Neal,' said Clover, beginning to understand, 'You were the first two to sign up for this weekend and you were both helping Lord Swann with publicity.'

The branches thickened overhead as the track bent around a mighty oak. Many of its leaves were still green, reaching towards the silvery autumn sunlight. Its roots had broken through the flattened mud of the track and Clover stepped over them with care, looking back at the ponies.

Tony was trudging just ahead of the two faithful steeds; he glanced up and gave her a nod.

Clover paused, preoccupied with seeing the horses negotiate the roots successfully while their indifferent young riders beamed and stared around at the woods in wonder.

'I don't know much about Neal, I'd never heard of him before this weekend,' said Clover, sounding interested to find out more.

'I don't know much more than you do,' said Zuzie. 'We only met once before yesterday for a weekend when we both came here to talk to William about his plans. He was the answer to William's prayers. It was like he appeared out of nowhere, eager and ready to help.'

'How did Lord Swann come to meet Neal?'

'I'm not sure but he certainly was quite a find. His credentials were excellent. He even carried his diplomas with him. He'd just got back from Boston and he was full of ideas.'

'Ideas about *Mind-Robics*, I presume. Did he show any of the materials to you?'

'No, he said he had to be strict about the licensing terms or the publishers would sue him.'

'I suppose that does sound like the kind of thing that might happen,' said Clover thoughtfully. 'What did you think of him, though?'

Zuzie blushed, 'He was very charming at first, very interesting to talk to. He was very attentive, it seemed like he was really interested in what I had to say.'

'About education?' asked Clover.

'About everything but a lot of things about teaching too. I think he'd been away for a long time and he had some catching up to do.'

'He didn't talk about where he'd been?'

'Not really, he was so interested when he was asking me questions that I don't think I asked him anything much.'

'Were you close?' asked Clover.

‘I only met him once before yesterday and I didn’t really care for that beard,’ said Zuzie. ‘But I suppose I was hopeful that if the weekend went well I’d see more of him,’ she shuddered thinking of what had happened. ‘I should be acting more horrified than this but it doesn’t seem very real to me.’

‘Take it from me, that’s exactly what it feels like when something like this happens,’ said Clover. Should you really be out here with us just now? Do you want to head back?’

‘No, it’s lovely to be among the children and out in the woods. It’d be worse stuck in my room. Anyway, my dealings with Neal were completely professional. He was friendly and William was a bit overexcited about the chance of some business success but that’s all there was to it.’

They cleared the treeline and followed the trail out into a wide field of golden grasses. Tony called out behind them as Starbuck couldn’t resist going down for grass and wrenching up a few dry crispy stalks from the ground. Tony tugged on his bridle but Starbuck only snorted as he chewed on his prize.

Stubb kept his head up obediently and Holly, who was riding him, reached forward to pat his neck. ‘Dumb animals,’ muttered Tony as he led the ponies onwards again.

‘They have better self control than most of us,’ said Zuzie over her shoulder. ‘Imagine if you were walking through a field full of savoury treats and there was no good reason why you shouldn’t nibble them. Would you be able to control yourself?’

Tony didn’t even look up at her and Zuzie left him to it, striding ahead with Clover once more. ‘If that’s the best help he can afford then I can see why cousin William was so desperate for money,’ she said.

‘Would you really say he was desperate?’ asked Clover, keeping up the pace by taking longer strides.

‘Definitely,’ said Zuzie, looking out over the valley where Swann Hall stood and into the gullies and fields beyond it. ‘Look over there, can you see that grey mound, behind those trees?’

‘Yes, what is that?’ asked Clover, squinting against the low sun.

‘It’s several tonnes of gravel that my dear cousin picked up cheaply. He had a plan to spread a layer of it over the paddock and turn it into an enormous car park. He thought that more parking space was the only thing he needed to attract hundreds more visitors.’

‘It doesn’t look like it’s going very well,’ said Clover thoughtfully.

‘He bought the gravel about five years ago and he still hasn’t even managed to complete the car park.’

‘What happened?’

‘I think he just lost interest and started putting his money into something else. Can you see the little valley just past the lake? Look closer.’

Clover looked where Zuzie was pointing and she could see a strange sight. There was a stockade of neatly cut logs that looked green and overgrown even from that distance. Looking closer, Clover could see that the logs made up the wall of a small fort that occupied half of the tiny valley. A stream ran through the middle of it emerging through an arch to tumble over the short drop, forming a small waterfall.

‘William tried building an adventure playground down there but he didn’t do any research at all,’ said Zuzie. ‘The stream surges for almost half the year and even when it’s not flooding the damp rots away the ropes. I don’t think it was ever even open to visitors.’

‘The worst thing is that he doesn’t really care,’ said Zuzie. ‘He just blunders on into the next thing. It’s practically a family tradition. When you see Swann’s Folly you’ll see what I’m talking about.’ Zuzie turned to look up the hill they were climbing but there was nothing to be seen in that direction yet.

‘Do you think he’s going to be alright?’ asked Clover. ‘Lord Swann, I mean.’

‘After what happened last night, your class might very well be the last children to visit Swann Hall before it goes out of business.’ Zuzie shook her head, ‘I didn’t even get to share my ideas with anyone, not that it’s really important any more.’

Clover was quiet for a moment. Zuzie had been a mine of information and Clover hoped that Detective Marsh managed to learn half as much from the young South African as Clover had discovered.

Things were beginning to make more sense now she knew about Lord Swann’s money-making schemes. His expensive video camera and the strings he’d pulled to get the education consultants together was just one more interesting game for an aristocrat who liked the idea of starting businesses but never managed to finish anything.

However, nothing Clover had learned gave her much of a clue about who, if anyone, might have been involved in Neal’s death. The only certainty was that it seemed to be a terrible thing for everyone.

Clover was thoughtful before she spoke again, ‘It’s a small thing, I know, but maybe you could at least share your ideas with our class. I’d be fascinated to hear about what you’ve been working on and I’m sure the children would be too. It was something to do with animals, wasn’t it?’

Zuzie shrugged, ‘My work isn’t exactly *Mind-Robics* but I’ve got a few ideas that seem to have really helped children with their learning.’

‘Well I, for one, can’t wait to see what you’ve got to share,’ said Clover as they picked their way through the long grass.

Ellie, Bernard and the children had stopped to rest and they were all sitting on a rise in the hillside that gave them a clear view over the treetops below.

‘Has anyone been practising the storytelling game I taught you?’ asked Bernard and he was met by a forest of raised hands. ‘Who’s brave enough to share their story with the rest of us?

We can try to guess which character is the storyteller.' Most of the hands stayed raised in the air and few of them waved eagerly.

'Yes, you,' said Bernard, picking out Sabina from the knot of girls who were clustered around Olivia.

'Some animals only left their house for a little while but when they returned there was a rare and dangerous creature in their house. It had been lurking in their sleeping area and it had destroyed the place. It even ate their food while it was trying to steal something to eat.'

'That's great storytelling,' said Bernard. 'Now, hands up who can tell me what the story is and which character is the storyteller.' He chose Michael, one of the boys on the far side of the group, to answer.

'It's one of the three bears and the dangerous creature is Goldilocks,' he said. 'It was one of the bears telling the story because they thought that the girl in the story was dangerous even though she wasn't.'

'That is truly excellent,' said Bernard. 'This is a really good example of what some scientists call *Negativity Bias*. The storyteller, one of the bears, has had a bad experience with human beings. He got a shock when he found a girl sneaking around his den. Now it might be that the girl is harmless but the storyteller bear is making them seem very scary and dangerous just because they had one bad experience. If you were a bear listening to this story, what would you think of human beings?'

'That they're dangerous,' suggested Alfie.

'They're always breaking into your house and taking things,' offered Amina.

Bernard nodded, 'History is full of people telling stories about one group of people or another, so what should we think about when we listen to those stories?'

Sequoia put up her hand and Bernard picked her to speak, 'Even if nobody is telling lies on purpose, the story could still be wrong because of a person's experience.'

'Precisely!' cried Bernard. 'That is why, as historians, we need to look at who is writing the stories in the past and understand what kind of bias they might have. Negativity bias is just one kind of problem but there are dozens of others to look out for and think about. This is why it's so hard to find the truth and this is why it's so important to study history,' said Bernard proudly. 'You must always look at the evidence and not simply follow your instincts.'

'But I should add that bears do not actually live in family groupings at all,' added Zuzie as soon as Bernard had finished.

'Yes, yes, of course but that's quite beside the point,' said Bernard quickly.

'Well, not really,' replied Zuzie, 'As Miss Lightfoot and I were just discussing, my own ideas about learning come from treating animals with respect and that means not telling and retelling foolish and untruthful stories about them. It just confuses everything.'

'But it's only a metaphor!' said Bernard.

'It's making light of something really important,' said Zuzie sharply. She turned to the children, 'Who here has ever touched a cow?' She raised her own hand but not one of the class raised theirs. 'I know you have met two lovely ponies today but how about a pig, or a chicken?' Sequoia's hand went up at this but she was the only one.

'Why do we casually talk about bears walking around and wearing clothes and being like us? We say it's just a metaphor but it's exactly this kind of untruthfulness is part of everything that is wrong with the world.'

Clover hadn't expected Zuzie to take such a radical tack but she didn't exactly disagree with her and was fascinated to hear more. Bernard, on the other hand, looked displeased.

'You're missing the point, the animals in the story aren't the important thing,' he said.

'Exactly, that is the precise problem,' responded Zuzie. 'The bears in your stories seem to have very middle-class human concerns about their habitat. This is extremely misleading. Whilst North American Black Bears do live in close proximity to each other it is far more common for bears to be solitary creatures who require a lot of space to live healthy lives. If you wanted to talk about predatory animals that live in families, it would be far better to use the fox as an example. They live in families and they're very interesting creatures. Did you know that they often kill more prey than they can eat with the intention of hiding the food to ensure they have enough to eat in the coming weeks? Usually people characterise this behaviour as viciousness whereas, in fact, they are taking the opportunity to think ahead and plan for the future.'

'I'm well aware of the basic *facts* about wildlife,' said Bernard, through gritted teeth, 'but I'm drawing on a well-established tradition of storytelling to teach these children about bias in historical evidence.'

'It seems to me that you are ignoring your own principles though. What was the agenda of the people who created these animal stories? They ignored even the most basic facts about animals and used the poor creatures to harp on about whatever the moral of their story happens to be. What could be more arrogant?'

'I do understand what you mean,' said Bernard, who was getting very red in the face, 'but can't you see that I'm only using animal stories to try to get my point across? I could have used other fairy tales like Cinderella or Rumplestiltskin just as easily. As I said, this isn't really anything to do with animals at all.'

'Well maybe it should be,' said Zuzie. 'All human life depends on the natural world and we're foolish to teach children myths that cover this up.'

Bernard couldn't contain himself any longer, 'Now you're just talking a lot of politically correct nonsense!' he said. 'Are you suggesting we crowbar information about animals into every single lesson? Perhaps I should be careful not to mention to the children that I occasionally enjoy a beefburger, just in case I accidentally influence them into destroying the planet because they don't spend their entire time thinking about cows?'

There was a silence for a moment when all the children looked to see what Zuzie would say, 'If you'd really want to talk about beefburgers then I think this is going to be a much longer discussion,' she replied eventually. Bernard threw his hands up in the air in fury and turned away from Zuzie, muttering under his breath.

Clover caught Ellie's eye and gave her a nod. Ellie understood immediately and stepped forward to take over the discussion, smoothly drawing the children's attention away from Bernard. 'What a fascinating talk,' Ellie said. 'I'm so glad that we can explore ideas and think them through together. Has anyone got any questions?'

David, who was a quiet member of the class and rarely the first to ask a question, raised his hand. Ellie smiled warmly. David asked earnestly, 'How can you tell if a bear is lying?' The discussion between Zuzie and Bernard had left him baffled.

Bernard screwed up the paper he was carrying and turned back towards Zuzie, giving her a furious look before walking away from the group. Ellie started to deal with David's question as Clover hurried after Bernard. She was wondering whether his anger might have got the better of him the previous night when Neal had made fun of him in front of the other consultants.

Bernard started to march up the hill, putting some distance between him and the group below. He didn't look back when Clover called out to him but she continued to follow him, breaking into a jog to keep up. If there was ever a time to see what Bernard was really like, now was her chance.

Swann's Folly was a ruined tower that stood on its own at the very top of the hill. It looked ancient, as if it might have been built by a Roman legion to oversee the barbarian lands that surrounded it, but nothing could have been further from the truth.

Swann's Folly was a late-Victorian structure, built by Lord Swann's great-grandfather in an early attempt to attract wealthy tourists. It had been specially built to look like a ruin and had never had a proper roof or stairs to lead up to the top of the tower and, up close, it looked odd and awkwardly proportioned.

Bernard came to a halt at the entrance to the tower and Clover, slightly out of breath, approached him cautiously. 'Mr King, are you alright?' she asked. Without looking back at her Bernard's head dropped and he put his face in his hands. It took her a few moments to understand that he was crying and she rushed to his side.

'Please, don't mind me' he said, between sobs. 'I will be fine. I get these anxiety attacks sometimes and they always pass.'

'Don't worry,' said Clover gently. All the rage had vanished from him and he seemed very vulnerable and small.

'I have some medication,' said Bernard weakly, as he fumbled in his jacket pocket and produced a small bottle of pills. 'I usually try not to take them until the end of the day because they knock me out completely.'

'I'm so sorry,' Clover said. 'I shouldn't have pressed you into helping out with the children today.'

'It would have been fine, normally,' said Bernard shaking his head. 'But the news of what happened to that poor man was such a shock, I think it's made things worse.' Bernard shook his head and Clover walked him to the far side of the tower as the children started to make their way up the hill to join them.

'Do you need to sit down?' asked Clover.

'Yes, that's a good idea,' said Bernard, swallowing one of the tablets and sitting down on the mossy grass. He lay on his back with his feet flat on the floor and his knees up in the air.

'Does this happen whenever you get angry or frustrated?' asked Clover, sitting down beside him.

'More often than I'd like, yes.'

'Did it happen last night, after the argument with Neal?'

'Yes but it wasn't as bad as this and it didn't matter so much because I could go straight to bed.' Bernard looked up at Clover, 'I can imagine what you suspect. I did go straight to bed, you know. Ask Sophie if you have any suspicions about me. I certainly wasn't capable of sneaking out to a darkened storage shed and beating a younger man to death.'

'I wasn't accusing you of anything,' said Clover quickly.

'True, but the bias of your questioning was very clear, Miss Lightfoot. However, you're barking up the wrong tree with me I'm afraid. The doctors' notes that come with my prescription make it perfectly clear that I couldn't hurt a fly. If you're looking to find someone to replace Jacqui Scarfe as Detective Marsh's prime suspect then I'm afraid I won't be able to help you.'

'You're very astute, Mr King.' said Clover with a smile.

'You're very astute yourself, Miss Lightfoot,' said Bernard closing his eyes and taking a deep breath. 'I believe I'll recover presently if you don't mind just letting me lie here for a little while.'

'I don't mind at all, Mr King,' said Clover. 'I'll see that the children keep quiet while you rest.'

She left Bernard on the far side of the folly and went to see what the children were doing. Ellie had them all sitting on the grass with their sketchbooks, starting on drawings of the folly. Zuzie sat with a small group of girls who were attempting to capture a likeness of the two ponies who were munching on the long grass. Tony sat some distance away staring in the opposite direction from the children looking into the distance.

Ellie and Clover spoke in whispers while the children got on with their artwork. 'Well then, how's it going, *Madame Detective*?'

'*Ms Detective*, if you must,' said Clover. 'But I don't think I deserve the title at the moment.'

'You certainly have a talent for getting people talking. You must have found out something new.'

'Yes, lots of things,' said Clover. 'But I'm not sure how useful any of those things are. It turns out that Zuzie is Lord Swann's niece. Lord Swann is careless with his money and probably bankrupt. Zuzie and Neal helped him to persuade all of the other consultants into coming to this weekend's event but I don't see how that would give her a motive to murder Neal. As for Bernard, he has a medical condition that means that he has the strength of a kitten once he gets grumpy. I don't think any of this is going to help us get to the bottom of what happened last night.'

Ellie looked thoughtful, 'Well it sounds as if you've ruled out two possible suspects in the space of a couple of hours, I doubt Detective Marsh can say the same. That probably won't be much comfort to Jacqui Scarfe, right now.'

'No,' said Clover, 'judging by how tense it was when I looked in on them, I imagine that won't be any comfort at all.'

8

Clover let Zuzie lead the front of the group while she and Ellie helped Bernard walk back down to the house, making sure that he didn't stumble. The effects of his medication were quite obvious and though he was able to walk on his own, he looked very unsteady.

From the top of the hill, Swann Hall and all its attendant buildings looked like a model village. As the whole group headed back down to the edge of the woods, Clover could see several distant figures tramping along the shore of the boating lake. There were three buildings near the lake but one of them was now cordoned off with a boundary of fluttering yellow tape strung between stakes planted in the ground.

Clover shuddered. That must have been the building where Neal had died last night. Seeing it made it all seem very real to Clover once again.

Within the hour, everyone was back on the lawn at the front of Swann Hall where Inspector Marsh was waiting for them. 'Miss Lightfoot, a word if you please?' he came close and talked quietly to Clover as she shepherded the children across the grass.

'I'm rather taken up with my responsibilities at the moment,' Clover replied. 'You did say that the children have to come first, didn't you?'

'Indeed, but I'm afraid that won't do right now,' said Marsh, coldly. 'Please come with me.' Ellie looked worried but Clover was quick to reassure her as she followed Inspector Marsh towards the house. 'I'll see you at lunch,' she said to Ellie. 'Save me something, won't you?'

Marsh led the way back into the classroom. Jacqui was gone and now it was Clover's turn to face his questions.

'Miss Lightfoot,' Marsh began abruptly, 'your colleague Miss Robinson mentioned that you heard someone leaving the house late last night and that you then heard someone else following them outside. How was that possible from three floors above the ground when none of the other visitors reported hearing anything at all?'

'We had the window open,' said Clover, taken aback by Marsh's accusing tone. 'We were taking the night air.'

'But neither you nor Miss Robertson left your room again that night?'

'No, like Ellie said, we heard some people moving around but we didn't think much about it.'

'And what time was this?' asked Marsh. 'Please can you be as specific as possible with your answers, Miss Lightfoot.'

‘Probably about ten thirty. We were tired out after a long day,’ said Clover. ‘I’m sorry, have I done something to offend you, Inspector Marsh?’ Clover asked, gently addressing Marsh’s aggressive tone.

‘Not at all, Miss Lightfoot. This is how I do my job. I try not to make any assumptions and I ascertain all of the facts. So, in your own words, please tell me everything about the sounds that you heard.’

Clover paused to think. ‘There was a click, then a creak, perhaps a door with rusty hinges opening. Now I think about it, that must have been the sound of the French doors in the dining room, they were directly below us. Then I heard footsteps on the gravel and he was walking quite quickly.

‘*He?*’ asked Marsh.

‘I’m guessing it was a man, the footsteps sounded heavy’ said Clover.

‘Think about the sounds that you actually heard. Could it have been a woman?’ Clover thought about Jacqui. She worried that Marsh was jumping to conclusions about her but all she could do was to answer honestly.

‘I don’t know if it was a man or a woman. The person walked quickly and the gravel crunched loudly under their feet. At the time I presumed that it was Lord Swann heading back to his Lodge for the night.’

‘But you’re not sure about that?’ Marsh pressed her. Clover shook her head.

‘What happened next?’

‘We heard the same click and creak but there weren’t any footsteps this time. The person might have stepped off the path onto the lawn. If they’d done that, they wouldn’t have made a sound.’

‘As if they were trying not to be heard?’ asked Marsh.

‘That might have been the reason but I don’t know, of course,’ said Clover.

'You said that a second person might have followed the first, could that have been a woman?

'I don't know,' Clover shook her head. 'It's possible,' she admitted.

'Did you hear anything else? Like the sound of someone returning to the building?'

'No, I didn't,' said Clover, 'And we went to bed just afterwards, we were really tired.'

Marsh nodded. 'Were you aware that I asked for all the individuals on the premises to stay in their rooms today?'

'Unless they were needed to work with the children,' Clover added.

'Indeed, so perhaps you could tell me why you needed Miss Zuleika and Mr King to help you out this morning?' Marsh continued.

'Well, as you know, Mr Fish instructed me to take over from Mr Flint as class teacher and he had already planned for the class to take the ponies up to the top of Swann's Reach. Miss Zuleika is an expert in working with animals and she has a lifelong connection to Swann Hall. I'm sure Lord Swann must have told you that Zuzie is his cousin?' Marsh's features darkened. Clover noted that this particular piece of information must not have been mentioned by Lord Swann.

'What about Mr King?' asked Marsh, 'Why did you ask him to accompany you and the children when there were reports of him making threats towards the deceased last night?'

'Mr King is a professional with a great deal of teaching experience and I was very grateful for his help. To someone with little or no teaching experience it might appear that one or two teachers can manage everything but if anything unexpected happens, you need to have additional responsible adults to help out.'

Marsh seemed to be waiting to hear a better answer to his question. 'However,' continued Clover, 'I wouldn't have asked him to join us if I'd known about his condition.'

‘His condition?’

‘It’s probably best if you ask him about that in person,’ said Clover. ‘Suffice it to say that I don’t believe Mr King is a threat to anyone.’

Marsh watched Clover closely, ‘I’ll be asking everyone about everything that I deem relevant, Miss Lightfoot. I’m always surprised about the unexpected things I discover, about yourself for example...’

Clover met Marsh’s gaze and raised her eyebrows, ‘I’m sure I don’t know what you’re talking about Inspector Marsh.’

‘Your headteacher, Mr Fish, was very forthcoming about your involvement with the police just a few months ago.’

Clover sighed, ‘I simply made some observations. The detective in charge deserved all the credit.’

‘I’m quite sure he does,’ agreed Marsh. ‘What would you think of someone who wandered into your classroom and thought that they were able to take over your job?’

‘I’d say that it’s much more complicated than it looks,’ replied Clover, innocently. ‘It takes a great deal of experience to teach well and there’s always more to learn. There’s a lot that can go wrong very quickly if you don’t know what you’re doing.’ Clover paused and smiled, ‘But I understand what you’re getting at, Inspector Marsh. You’re suggesting that I shouldn’t involve myself in your investigation.’

‘All I’m suggesting, Miss Lightfoot, is that my investigation is a police matter. Years of experience are needed to look into something like this and there’s a lot that can go wrong if you don’t know what you’re doing.’

‘You have made your point, Detective Marsh,’ said Clover.

‘Have I?’ asked Marsh. ‘You are aware that obstructing a police officer, wasting police time and perverting the course of justice are all criminal activities, aren’t you?’

A knock at the door made Clover jump. ‘I believe that’s all for now, Miss Lightfoot,’ said Marsh, ‘but I may wish to speak to you again.’

The door opened and Tom walked into the room, looking far from well. ‘Tom,’ cried Clover. ‘What are you doing out of bed?’

‘I said I’d be talking to everyone,’ said Marsh. ‘Mr Flint is no exception.’

Clover glared at Marsh, ‘Why get Tom out of bed when he’s sick? He didn’t even meet Neal.’

‘Then I’m sure I’ll find nothing suspicious during my questioning, Miss Lightfoot. That’s all for now, please close the door on your way out.’

Clover turned to Tom, ‘You go straight back to bed when you’re done here and don’t let yourself get tired out.’

‘Don’t worry, I’ll be fine,’ Tom replied.

Clover gave his arm a friendly squeeze as she left the room and shut the door behind her, feeling rather piqued by her abrupt dismissal. She walked slowly along the corridor towards the dining room, trying to make sense of the conversation she had just had with Inspector Marsh.

‘Everything alright?’ asked Ellie, coming up behind her.

Clover jumped, still a little rattled from her encounter with Marsh. ‘I think I just got told off for not minding my own business.’

‘I wondered if that was it,’ said Ellie with a smile.

‘I don’t know what I was thinking, getting myself involved like this. Marsh can deal with this, it’s his job after all.’

‘I know what you were thinking. You were remembering how you averted a terrible miscarriage of justice just a few months ago,’ said Ellie firmly. ‘Don’t you start doubting yourself Clo. We’ve all had a weird shock this weekend and we’re coping with it as best we can.’

Clover melted at this and found a smile for her friend, ‘How are the sandwiches?’ she asked.

‘You can taste Lord Swann’s budgetary decisions in every bite but at least there’s plenty to go around. I’ll take the children out onto the lawn for some playtime so that you have a chance to eat in peace.

Clover filled up her paper plate with cheese and pickle sandwiches and collected a beaker of orange squash. She was so hungry that even a basic meal felt like a proper feast.

Jacqui Scarfe was sitting on the steps outside the French windows and, seeing her there, Clover abandoned the stuffy dining hall and headed outside to sit with Jacqui in the warm afternoon sunshine.

'Hi,' said Clover cautiously. Jacqui looked subdued after her interview with Inspector Marsh. 'Mind if I join you?' she asked.

'Oh, please do!' said Jacqui, shuffling along the step to give Clover room to sit beside her. She was watching a group of the boys kicking a football around the lawn, happily absorbed in their game.

'It all seems so simple when you watch them playing doesn't it?'

'Maybe we think about everything too much,' said Clover, thinking again of Marsh's warning to stay away from the investigation.

'No, I don't think that's true,' said Jacqui firmly. 'We mustn't let it become wrong to speak out about what we see going on around us, no matter what the consequences are.'

'Consequences?' asked Clover.

'I never imagined that speaking my mind would lead to someone interrogating me over a murder,' said Jacqui. 'It's unthinkable. I didn't know whether to be terrified or offended.'

'If it's any consolation, I really agree with what you said last night,' said Clover. 'Some of these people are parasites. The arrangements for in-service training for teachers are appalling. It's mostly either money-for-old-rope or complete nonsense. How did it get like this?'

'I suspect that part of the reason is that teachers don't have any time to read anything any more,' said Jacqui, bleakly.

‘When was the last time you had a couple of hours to reflect on your classroom practice?’

Clover shrugged. The thought of having any time to sit and think without the pressure of assessing, marking and planning was completely unlikely.

‘I’ve read your books,’ she said. They’re really worth spending time on. *Conversations for Learning* changed my world.’

‘You’re very kind,’ said Jacqui.

‘I love the way it’s all about using the power of talk to extend children’s learning and how learning is reciprocal,’ said Clover. ‘When a child answers a question that you’ve asked them, I always try to fully engage with that answer rather than just tell them that they are right or wrong. As teachers, I’ve always felt we need to listen properly when children talk.’

‘I couldn’t agree with you more,’ said Jacqui, ‘That’s why the lessons that are planned with absolute precision often don’t really help children to learn at all, there’s no place for a meaningful dialogue.’

‘You’re preaching to the choir,’ said Clover, admiringly, ‘I just wish I could convince everyone else to see the light. You’re a pioneer.’

‘To be honest, some of these ideas have been around for many years. Bakhtin and Vygotsky, were the real pioneers, they were both born in the 1890s, although their ideas didn’t reach us here till much later. But essentially the idea that teachers should simply broadcast information and facts to children in their classrooms is a very difficult one to dislodge, even in the 1990s.’

‘Well, I’m grateful that you’re trying to move things on for the teaching profession,’ said Clover. ‘It might not be a quick fix but it could really make a difference to thousands of children’s lives.’

'Would you like a job in public relations?' said Jacqui, laughing. 'You might be the only person in the world with a chance of convincing teachers to buy my book.'

'Your real problem is that you haven't *productised* your work enough,' said a cool, sharp voice from behind them, causing Clover to choke slightly on her sandwich. Jeremy Billingham was standing at the French windows looking down at them.

'*Productised*?' asked Jacqui, doubtfully. Clover took a gulp of orange squash as Mr Billingham slid past her to perch on the steps beside Jacqui.

'Nobody's going to buy an expensive tome that they'll need to spend months deciphering,' he said. 'If you want to sell more of your work then you're going to have to turn it into a better *product*. Make it more accessible and at least give your readers a *pressé* of your work.'

'Are you talking about feeding books into a juicer or do you mean *précis*?' asked Clover.

'Either...both...take your pick,' replied Mr Billingham lightly, shrugging off Clover's comment. 'The point is that your ideas are probably fabulous but your audience can't tell at a glance if they're any good, so they're not going to buy it.'

'That might just be because it requires some effort to learn something new,' said Clover, unable to stop herself.

Billingham ignored her and spoke directly to Jacqui. 'I'm Jeremy Billingham, I was a management consultant before I became a teacher, so I know what I'm talking about.'

'Just what are you suggesting?' asked Jacqui.

'Well, to be brutally honest,' said Billingham, 'if you want to become as big as Gryffin Parr you probably need to get off your high horse about theories and focus on what you're able to sell. Think about techniques and pre-planned lessons that you could write up for teachers to buy. Try to move away from the theoretical side of things and make what you're offering more practical.'

Clover couldn't have disagreed more, 'With Jacqui's work, learning about the ideas is what's important. It's more subtle than just throwing teachers a lesson plan.'

'You may have a problem there,' said Billingham. 'It doesn't really matter how good your ideas are; they could be the best ideas in the world but if you don't turn them into a *toolkit* for teachers to use then you're not going to sell many books. The same goes for in-service training. You can't just expect to go around telling teachers about your books any more. You need some kind of a *signature activity* that teachers can learn and copy when they work with their classes. That's the kind of thing I look for when I'm booking someone to lead a training day. Something *real* that teachers can be seen to be doing, something that I can be proud of as a school leader and, frankly, something that makes us look good to Ofsted.'

Clover was appalled, 'So you think that training should be focused on making the school management look good, regardless of how much it affects the children?'

'I'm just saying that's the reality of how this business works. You don't have to like it but you can't deny it's true.'

'It shouldn't be,' said Clover bitterly. 'We should all think more carefully about what we're doing.'

Billingham paused and looked past Jacqui to stare at Clover, as if he'd only just noticed she was there. 'Mr Fish has been making arrangements to send the children home but there are one or two parents that we can't reach, perhaps you could go and assist him in the office, Miss Lightfoot?'

Clover's jaw dropped at being dismissed like this but reluctantly she got to her feet and managed to give Jacqui a smile.

'It was lovely to meet you.' Clover said, 'Your ideas are amazing and I'm sure the profession will recognise that sooner or later.'

'That recognition might come a great deal sooner if you invested in a good promotional video,' chipped in Billingham, conversationally. 'I think what Lord Swann was trying to do this weekend had some real merit, don't you?' Jacqui gave Clover a sympathetic wave of thanks as Clover retreated in the direction of the office where Mr Fish would be waiting for her.

9

Mr Fish was sitting at a desk in the small office by the main staircase with a copy of the class list in front of him.

'Ah, Clover! Do you have any idea why I can't reach any of these parents? I've rung most of them twice already but there's no reply.'

'I suppose they might be out for the day. Have you left messages for them?'

'None of them seem to have answerphones,' replied Mr Fish, obviously frustrated with his task. Clover looked down the list at the names without ticks next to them: Jake, Josh, Olivia, Holly, Chloe and Sequoia. Mr Fish sighed. 'I can't send these children back if there's nobody there to collect them. If I can't get hold of them by the end of the afternoon, we might be stuck with these six overnight.'

'We can certainly look after six of them without too much difficulty,' said Clover.

'They'll be in good company, that's for sure,' said Mr Fish, 'Inspector Marsh is adamant that all of the teachers and consultants will need to remain in the vicinity until he's finished his investigation.'

'Hold on though, if all the teachers have to stay, who's going to supervise the children on the coach journey home?' asked Clover.

'I've already thought of that,' said Mr Fish. 'Miss Morrison from Year Two is driving out this afternoon. She'll leave her car here and ride back with the children to see that they all get collected.'

'Well done,' said Clover, 'that does sound sensible.'

'Could you and Ellie start getting the children ready to go? The coach will be here within the hour.'

'Of course, right away,' said Clover, suddenly feeling gloomy at the prospect of being at Swann Hall without the children. 'And what shall we tell the children whose parents aren't available?'

'Tell them to get ready with the others for now and I'll keep trying to get through to them,' said Mr Fish, 'but perhaps you and Ellie could figure out a rota between the two of you to look after them for the evening. Tom doesn't seem to be any better and we want maximum attendance at this evening's meetings with the consultants.'

'What?' asked Clover. 'Surely we're not continuing with the lectures after what's happened?'

'Well, life must go on,' said Mr Fish firmly. Lord Swann is very keen to film some more of the sessions and I'm in agreement with Mr Billingham about the matter; we might as well make the best of the opportunity. Despite Inspector Marsh's suspicious mind, I'm inclined to think that the unfortunate demise of Mr Skinner will turn out to be nothing more than a tragic accident.'

'Really? What makes you say that?' asked Clover, surprised.

'Apart from a very minor squabble with the other teaching consultants, I don't see that anyone has any motive for murder. No, I rather suspect Mr Skinner went for an unwise rummage, looking for resources and he simply had a very awkward fall.'

'I suppose that's possible. I hope you're right,' said Clover as she turned to go. Perhaps it was simply an accident? If that was the case then at least she didn't have to worry about Jacqui Scarfe being wrongly accused and that would be good news. Maybe those troubling incidents during the school inspections last year had left her paranoid. Either that, or everyone but Inspector Marsh wasn't quite paranoid enough.

Clover made her way straight outside to pass on the news about the timings for the coach to Ellie and the children.

'We're trying to send everyone home today,' said Clover to the class, 'which is a day earlier than planned.' The children watched her quietly, absorbing this information. 'Mr Fish is going to write a letter to everyone's parents explaining the reason why in more detail but there's nothing for any of you to worry about.'

'So why do we have to go?' asked Noah who was part of Josh's gang. 'It was just starting to get fun.'

'It's a change of plan that is beyond our control so we'll need to make the best of it.'

'Did we do something wrong?' asked Holly, forgetting to put her hand up.

'No, of course not,' said Clover. 'It's nothing like that. This is more like finding out that it's going to rain tomorrow and changing our plans so we don't get stranded in the middle of a storm.'

'We could wear the rainproof things if it's going to be wet,' suggested Chloe.

'No,' Clover shook her head. 'I was using that as an example but it's nothing to do with the weather. It is something that we can't change right now, so let's see if we can get used to the idea together. Who can imagine something really positive about going home early?' Hands went up and Clover picked a few people to answer.

'I get to see my dog *Brewster* tonight,' said David.

'That's a great positive thing,' said Clover, approvingly. 'Thank you David. Yes, Charles, have you got one?' Clover pointed to another boy.

‘I get to see David’s dog tonight too,’ said Charles. ‘He’s a Labrador puppy,’ he explained, as if this added significant weight to his argument.

‘Another excellent reason,’ said Clover, unable to resist a smile. ‘Does anyone have a positive reason for going home that isn’t related to spending time with David’s dog?’

The way the children saw everything was so immediate. Clover knew that if she could keep them focused on positive things then the departure could go very smoothly after all. She elicited a few more ideas about the delights of home: snacks, home-cooked food and favourite television shows. Soon Clover’s activity was working so well that she was beginning to feel a little envious of the children herself.

Within half an hour, a line of suitcases and rucksacks were stacked up along the edge of the lawn in anticipation of the coach’s arrival.

A small blue mini crunched across the gravel and parked beside the main building. Clover recognised Simone Morrison behind the wheel and headed over to say hello. Simone Morrison seemed to radiate an energetic disposition no matter what was thrown at her.

‘Hey, what’s up, Clo?’ she asked as Clover approached.

‘Mr Fish didn’t tell you? You should probably ask him to explain, if that’s alright.’

‘Hmm, sounds very mysterious, but no worries,’ said Simone with a grin, ‘I’ll get all the gossip from Ellie anyway. Do you know who’s supposed to be driving my car back?’ Simone dangled the keys in the air.

‘I’ll can take care of it if you like,’ Clover offered, holding out her hand.

‘That’s what I was hoping to hear,’ said Simone handing her the keys. ‘No offence to anyone else but I’d sooner leave it with you than old Fishy or the new guy.’ Clover couldn’t help but smile at the way Simone referred to Mr Fish and Mr

Billingham. Simone was a complete professional but she didn't have much patience with the school's leadership and she often compared Mr Fish's approach to that of her previous headteacher back in Melbourne.

'She's a good little runner and her tank's full, she shouldn't give you any problems,' continued Simone, patting the roof of the car with obvious pride.

'I'll take care of her but I hope you don't need her back soon. I'm not sure when we'll be coming back yet,' said Clover.

'What, seriously? What's going on?' Simone asked, surprised.

'Perhaps you should see how much gossip you really can get out of Ellie,' said Clover carefully as she spied Mr Fish coming out of the main entrance and coming their way.

'Right you are,' said Simone jogging off towards Ellie before Mr Fish reached them.

'Why didn't you tell Simone what happened?' Clover asked Mr Fish as he approached.

'The fewer people who know the whole story, the better,' said Mr Fish. 'If it turns out to have been an accident then it might not even get into the news and we could say it was all just an administrative problem.'

'That's doesn't sound right to me,' said Clover warily. 'I'd suggest being as honest with the parents as possible, as quickly as possible. I told the children you'd be writing their parents a letter.'

'Yes, yes, quite right,' said Mr Fish, backtracking. 'For now, let's just see about getting as many of them back home as we can. I still can't get hold of the parents of those last six children so it looks like they'll be staying the night after all.'

At that moment a coach swayed up the drive and parked with a loud hiss.

At the same moment Lord Swann emerged from the inside the Lodge. He cut a jovial figure as he trotted across the lawn, carrying a large bowl of lollipops. The children spied him coming and swarmed over to him, clustering eagerly around the bowl and grabbing at the lollies. Whenever a particular flavour didn't appeal, they threw them back and dived in for another one, causing chaos. Ellie went across to try to restore order.

Clover shook her head as she watched, 'What's Lord Swann playing at? Giving the children a lot of sugar before a long coach ride probably isn't a great idea.'

'I'm sure it can't do any harm,' Mr Fish replied dismissively.

At that moment there was a howl from several of the children as it emerged that the unthinkable had happened. The lollipops had run out. As even the less popular flavours were snatched up it was apparent that there weren't enough to go around.

Clover rushed over to intervene as several of the children who'd been waiting more politely to choose a treat started to realise that they were going to miss out.

'Didn't you check there were enough lollies for everyone before you started giving them out?' Clover asked Lord Swann, seeing the disappointment on several faces.

'Ha ha! Well, no,' he said merrily, 'I just saw them lying round and I suddenly thought that it seemed a shame not to give them out. Waste not want not, eh?'

'But what about the children who've missed out?' asked Clover. 'It's not very fair on them.

Lord Swann puffed his cheeks, 'Well, the little blighters should probably get used to the idea that life's not fair. Bit of a lesson in the ways of the world and all that isn't it?'

Clover stared at him exasperated, unsure of where to begin, 'Have you spent much time actually working with children yourself, Lord Swann?' she asked.

He laughed again at this, 'Haw! Not if I can help it, eh?'

'Well that much is clear,' said Clover. She turned to the children, some of whom were parading the deliciousness of their lolly under the noses of those who had missed out.

‘If you didn’t get a lolly today then I’m sorry about that, I’ll make sure that anyone who missed out will get two lollies when we’re all back at school together. And if you did happen to get one, please say thank you to Lord Swann.’

There were muted noises of acceptance from the children who had lost out and attempts at thanks from some of the others. Clover grimaced. Allowing little acts of unfairness to occur when working with a group like this could encouraging all kinds of anxieties and bad habits. Lord Swann wandered off back into the house, smilingly oblivious to the effect of his actions.

Clover now had another awkward task to perform. ‘Could the following children come over and have a chat with me for a moment please: Jake, Josh, Holly, Chloe, Olivia and Sequoia.’ Clover seated the little group together on the grass. ‘Now, we have phone numbers to contact all your parents but I just checked with Mr Fish and we weren’t able to get through to them yet. Do any of you know why that might be?’

She was met by a few blank looks before Olivia suggested that her parents had been talking about going to visit her granddad. None of the other children had any idea where their parents might be.

‘We can’t send you home if there’s nobody there to look after you when we get there, can we?’ said Clover. ‘So if you’d like to go and collect your bags from the pile then we’ll look after you here until we can contact your parents.’

‘You mean we get to stay?’ asked Josh gleefully.

‘You mean we can’t go home?’ asked Olivia, looking alarmed.

‘I know it’s not exactly fair,’ said Clover, wishing again that it wasn’t the second example of unfairness that the children had been shown in the last few minutes. ‘But it’s just a matter of what’s possible at the moment.’

‘What’s happened?’ asked Sequoia, looking serious. Clover could see she had guessed that something was wrong. The others hadn’t caught up yet but they were unsettled too.

‘We’ll have a big talk about it later but look at it this way. You get a special adventure and me and Miss Robertson will both be here to look after you the whole time.’ Sequoia nodded thoughtfully at this, content to save her questions for now.

About fifteen minutes later, the coach pulled away with Tom’s class waving enthusiastically at the six children left behind and some started thumping on the window, a move that was swiftly curtailed by the capable Simone on the coach. If trips like this were intended to bring the class together as a group, much of that work had been undone by the circumstances of their departure and Lord Swann’s carelessness. It left Clover feeling a little drained.

‘Do you want to take the first shift with the children?’ asked Ellie generously. ‘I’ll go along to the meeting and you can stay out here.’ Clover looked around. The six who remained behind were a very different kettle of fish from the thirty lively children who they had been supervising over the weekend. Sequoia had pulled a huge novel from her bag and she sat propped up against her rucksack reading quietly. Olivia and Chloe were deep in conference, casting occasional glares across towards Holly, who was playing tag with Josh and Jake and running about wildly. Taking care of a group like this would be a pleasure.

It was much easier to see them as individuals now that there were fewer of them. However, Clover could see potential trouble ahead: Smaller groups could grow tired of each other more quickly without other children around to give them a break from each other’s company. There was a chance that they’d become more fractious as the evening went on and they got bored with each other. Clover reflected that perhaps sometimes it could be much easier to manage a group of thirty children then it was to manage a group of six.

‘Would you mind taking them for now, Ellie?’ said Clover. ‘I’ll go and sit in on whatever is being talked about by the so-called grown-ups. I won’t have the patience to face it later on and I’ll be happy to take the lead in getting these guys off to sleep when the time comes.’

Ellie nodded and gave her friend a broad smile. She was obviously relieved not to have to go back indoors. ‘Leave this lot to me,’ she said. ‘I can wait a little longer to hear what the next exciting lecture is about. Let me guess, something like *How to cause trouble in the classroom without really trying*?’

‘Nope, I don’t think that’s been quite *productised* enough,’ said Clover.

‘What?’ asked Ellie, ‘What does that mean?’

‘Believe me,’ said Clover wearily, ‘You definitely don’t want to know.’

10

When Clover arrived back at the classroom, Inspector Marsh had packed away his things and was about to leave. Sophie King stood at the front, ready to lead the next session and the consultants and teachers were settling in their seats. Marsh gave the occupants of the room a final, suspicious glance as he walked to the door.

‘Thank you all for your cooperation,’ he said, ‘and thank you also for agreeing to stay here until the investigation is concluded. I do hope you all have a pleasant evening.’ He looked around once more as if he doubted that would be the case. ‘We will continue the investigation in the morning.’

Sophie had moved the desks around so that people could work in pairs. Bernard and Zuzie were sitting together and seemed to be getting on in a friendly way after their hike up the hill with Clover and the ponies. Simon Fish and Julie Giroux, on the other hand, looked rather uncomfortable in each other's company. Julie's dignified elegance seemed to be quite intimidating to poor Mr Fish and he was fussing over the large pieces of sugar paper and felt tip pens on the desk in front of them.

Jeremy Billingham was sitting with Jacqui Scarfe, still relentlessly badgering her about consultancy techniques. That left Gryffin Parr, the most high-profile of the consultants, sitting on his own. Clover took the seat next to him and they exchanged a brief smile. Gryff stretched his legs under the desk and appeared to be rather bored.

'Alright then, everyone!' boomed Lord Swann from the back of the room. He had been setting up his video camera and the large machine on a heavy tripod tooted a short melody. He switched on the arc light and asked, 'Everyone ready?' Without waiting for a response he declared, 'Time to get on with the show. Lights, camera and action!'

Sophie made a good job of ignoring the camera and offered everyone a bold smile. 'Welcome to my session about *Emotionally Motivated Learning*. We're going to explore a few ideas about how our feelings affect how and what we learn. I'd like to start with a little activity to get us all thinking about our emotions.' She produced a large sand timer and set it firmly on the desk. 'For the next five minutes, I'd like you all, in your pairs, to make a list of everything that you can think of that makes you happy. Also, could you indicate which items on the list you have in common with your partner. Off you go!'

The room started to fill with chatter. Gryff turned to Clover and handed her a pen. 'Sport is way up there for me,' he said at once, 'wine and food too, *physical pleasures* are an important source of happiness, don't you think?' Gryff gave her a salacious wink, and pointed to the centre of the sheet of paper, where he expected her to write his ideas.

Clover wrote the words but ignoring his wink, shifted uncomfortably in her seat. 'How about *music*?' she suggested. 'I discovered a perfect album a few weeks ago. It's called *Tigermilk* and it's by a funny little Scottish band. They took their name from a TV show I used to watch when I was tiny about a boy and a dog. I never imagined that music that sounds so wistful could make me feel so happy.'

Gryff sighed at this, 'I think it would probably be best to think in terms of big categories, not specific little details.' He took the pen from her hand and wrote *music* in tiny letters at the edge of the paper in a way that could hardly be more dismissive.

Clover defiantly picked up another pen and wrote *Belle and Sebastian* in larger letters underneath it. Gryff scowled, 'Don't you think that's way out of proportion compared with the other things we were talking about?' he asked.

Clover smiled, 'Well, you haven't listened to *Belle and Sebastian*, have you?' she replied.

'Fair enough,' said Gryff, writing a few more items in the middle of the paper without another word to her. Clover sat back in her chair and let him get on with it. Gryff added *films, a fine cigar* and *cricket*, to his short list of words.

Picking up her own pen again, Clover wrote, *reading (evening), chocolate* and *time with friends*, on her side of the page.

'Time's up,' declared Sophie. 'Who would like to share their work first?' Bernard and Zuzie had constructed a Venn diagram, with words scattered across both circles and the overlapping arc in the middle. They held up their piece of paper together and took it in turns to explain what they'd written.

'That looks absolutely marvellous,' Sophie declared as she appraised their diagram. 'And that's a fantastic way of setting it out too, I might ask everyone to do that in future. I like it because it really emphasises the things that this pair have in common.' Sophie read through the words, 'French cinema, the outdoors, vegan food.' she paused, giving her husband a curious look. 'Really Bernard? *Vegan food?* That's news to me.' Sophie had treated Bernard with no more familiarity than anyone else in the room until that moment and Clover had quite forgotten that Sophie and Bernard were married.

'Well, whatever exciting things you've discovered,' said Sophie with a dismissive wave of her hand, 'I'd like you to teach each other something new about one of the things that makes you both happy, then I'll ask you to feed back about how that went.'

Clover looked at the large piece of sugar paper that she shared with Gryff. It looked very bare compared to the one belonging to Bernard and Zuzie. Clover felt disappointed in herself, she usually loved collaborating in activities but she couldn't quite bring herself to engage with Gryff, who seemed completely self-centred. She resolved to make an additional effort to join in the spirit of the exercise and she looked down the Gryff's list.

'I love films too,' she offered, 'and I was interested in what you were saying in your talk about thinking like a hero in a story.'

Gryff brightened at this, 'Yes, that's what I think is really important about movies,' he said. 'Like Tom Cruise in that new *Mission Impossible* film, you have to find the truth, no matter what it takes.'

Clover grinned, 'Or like that other Tom Cruise film *Jerry Maguire,* where the hero's just as lost as everyone else but he keeps pretending he knows what he's doing.'

'No, you're missing the point completely,' declared Gryff.

'Why do I feel like the more we talk the less we're going to agree on anything?' asked Clover, trying to find some humour in the situation.

'Maybe it's because you're only a teacher and not a consultant,' said Gryff seriously. 'I have to say, I thought this event was going to be a bit more selective about who they invited along. I suppose you're not really to blame, they've only dragged you in here to make up the numbers, after all.'

'*Only* a teacher?' asked Clover, incredulous at his rudeness.

'Well, you know what I mean, you're just here to soak up advice and learn as much as you can from the experts before you go back to the daily grind.'

Clover struggled to keep her temper in check. 'I'm here because I'm an experienced practitioner who's dedicated to her work,' she said. 'It's true that I'm not trying to sell anything to anyone but I'm also not so arrogant that I'd claim to know better than everyone else. If there's one thing I've learned from years of teaching, it is that how you approach working with the children is just as important as any theory or practices you might adopt along the way.'

'Can we all come back together again now?' said Sophie. 'Who's got a good example of something you've discovered that makes both you and your partner happy?'

Gryff spoke up at once, 'We discovered that we're both big fans of Tom Cruise,' he said smoothly, as if they hadn't had the tiniest disagreement. 'I think it really helped us to connect. My young colleague here was just telling me how excited she was about my theory of *The Heroic Journey.*' Clover was speechless.

'Anything to add? It's *Miss Lightfoot* isn't it?' asked Sophie. Clover didn't know where to begin. Gryff was arrogant and rude but he also knew how to handle an audience. He hadn't actually lied about what they'd talked about but he'd characterised everything in a way that made it very hard for her to challenge him.

'I'm not sure what I can add in the context of this exercise,' said Clover, thinking quickly. 'Except to say that Gryff has certainly shown me what it's like for him to be very much the hero of his own story.'

There was a slightly uncomfortable silence as everyone tried to work out whether this was a compliment or an insult. Clover allowed herself a secret smile and Sophie moved on swiftly.

Jeremy Billingham talked at some length about how he'd discovered that Jacqui Scarfe loved Lewis Carroll as much as he did. Through a torturous connection, this then led him to explain the necessity of teaching the Oxford comma to children before they went into Year 2. Jacqui didn't seem to have anything to say about this.

Before Sophie could continue, Julie Giroux raised her hand. 'Is the point of this exercise simply to encourage teachers to talk to children about what they enjoy?' she asked in a sceptical tone. 'Because I understand that teachers endeavour to do this as much as possible already.'

'My point,' said Sophie, 'is that it may make a qualitative difference to children's learning if we strive to talk to children about things that make them happy.'

'But if you are correct, how are teachers supposed to use this knowledge to help them teach?'

'That's where you come in, actually,' said Sophie, brightly. 'I thought that we could all brainstorm our ideas for how children could use this to make a difference to their work...'

'...then once we have shared our ideas, will you be putting them all in a booklet so that you can sell them to teachers?' asked Julie Giroux bitterly. 'My dear girl, if only you knew how many times I've been in a session where we all had to *brainstorm* ideas for *this, that* or *the other thing*. Don't you have some original thoughts of your own to contribute or did you expect us to do all your work for you?'

Sophie looked flustered. Bernard came to his wife's defence, although he did so rather blusteringly. 'Come now Julie, we're all colleagues here. Surely we're able to pool our thoughts from time to time. Requesting a group discussion is a perfectly legitimate way of exploring an idea. AF Osborne came up with a procedure for collectively generating ideas as early as 1939.'

'Honestly Bernard,' replied Julie, sounding very tired, 'you and Sophie do make quite a pair. You know far too much to be of use to anyone and she knows far too little.' Sophie gasped and a deathly silence fell over the room.

'And cut!' declared Lord Swann, his video camera beeped a concluding fanfare. 'I do believe we're out of time for this evening.' Gryff chuckled rather too loudly at Lord Swann's attempt to avoid any more conflict and Sophie turned and walked out of the room. She was followed closely by Bernard and the meeting broke up in confusion.

Clover slipped away quickly too, heartily relieved to be making her way back to Ellie and the remaining children.

11

The evening was already beginning to draw in and Clover was surprised to find that Ellie and the children were still outside on the lawn. She didn't waste any time in hurrying out to meet them as they sat calmly in the twilight. As Clover approached their small circle, Olivia and Jake shuffled aside to make a space for her to join them.

'Miss Robinson is telling us a ghost story,' said Jake with an excited smile.

'Now Jake,' said Ellie, 'remember what I just said. There are definitely no such things as ghosts. We all know that, we're just discussing some of the history about Hatton Hoo. It's almost the opposite of a ghost story.'

'Still, that sounds a very...*appropriate*...subject to start this late in the evening,' said Clover, pitching her sarcasm mildly enough so that only Ellie would notice. 'I hope we'll all be able to sleep well after this.'

'Don't worry Miss Lightfoot, I was told these very same stories when I visited here as a little girl,' said Ellie, with a smile. 'It didn't do me any harm.' She changed tone to address

Clover directly, 'Besides, it was the best way of obfuscating our current circumstances.'

Clover raised an eyebrow at this. Ellie was choosing her words carefully and Clover could guess why. As teachers they constantly structured their language to engage the children's attention. If necessary, they could just as easily use the same adjustments to do the opposite and talk about necessities using a vocabulary and style of speech that the children wouldn't bother to follow.

'I take it that you had queries from our little congregation about the constabulary?' asked Clover over the children's blank looks.

'Suspicions that never burgeoned into an inquisition,' Ellie replied slyly. 'Not once I presented a suitable diversion, anyway.'

The children looked as if they had tuned out from their teachers' conversation. As far as they were concerned, the adults were simply doing some of their grown-up business and it was probably far too boring to be worth following.

'I support your decision completely,' said Clover with a smile. 'Do proceed and if you're wrong, we'll just have to count the cost in hours of slumber.'

'My thoughts exactly,' said Ellie.

'Now, who can point out Hatton Hoo to Miss Lightfoot?' she asked the children, re-engaging with them again. Six hands shot up and pointed to the misshapen, conical hill in the distance.

'That's right,' said Ellie. 'That hill isn't a natural feature, it was made by people with their bare hands, people who lived a very, very long time ago in what we call the *neolithic* era, that's about twelve thousand years ago. Hatton Hoo is what we call a *barrow,* which is a very old word for a hill or a mountain.'

Clover chipped in, 'You remember studying the ancient Romans with me last year? Well, the Romans came to Britain about *two* thousand years ago. So Hatton Hoo was sitting over there, looking like that, for *ten* thousand years before the Romans even arrived in Britain.'

A hush fell over the group. Ellie carried on, 'Would anyone like to guess what it's for?'

'Burying people, like the pyramids in Egypt,' suggested Chloe with a bloodthirsty smirk.

'You're quite right,' said Ellie. 'The people who built Hatton Hoo might have had similar ideas to the people who built the pyramids, we don't know for sure. We do know what's inside though,' said Ellie. 'I'm going to need some volunteers to show you properly.' All of the children put their hands up at once.

'Sequoia, would you play the part of the ancient king?' asked Ellie. Sequoia nodded and Ellie directed her to lie down in the middle of the circle.

'When the great king died,' whispered Ellie, 'the prince organised the burial.' Ellie pointed at Olivia, picking her to play the part of the prince. 'We believe that the prince buried the great king with all his finest treasures. They buried him inside one of his finest boats, a boat with strong wooden sides,' she said.

'Here's the treasure,' said Ellie tossing her cardigan to Sequoia. 'You two can be the sides of the boat,' she said, as she picked Holly and Chloe out of the circle. The two girls knelt at each side of Sequoia and Olivia, then Ellie got them to put their arms out to the sides, as if to make the protective shape of a boat's sides.

Ellie nodded her approval before she continued, 'We think that the prince must have ordered the people to work for days and months to cover up the dead king and the ship completely with a huge hill of rocks and earth, burying them completely.'

'Jake, Josh, can you two be the hillsides?' she asked. The boys jumped to join in lifting up their arms to make an arch over Sequoia and the other children.

'That's it,' said Ellie. 'Now, if a *thief* came along trying to steal the treasure. I bet you'd be able to stop that from happening.' Ellie slowly got to her feet and with theatrical stealth she moved closer to where the children were playing their parts, as if she were trying to avoid being spotted. There were excited grins on the children's faces as they realised what the game was.

Ellie moved ever more slowly and whispered as she went, 'Even the most cunning thief would have to dig down through the whole hill or smash their way in through the sides of the boat to get at the...'

'Treasure!' finished Clover who had been creeping up on the far side of the children while Ellie distracted them. Clover stole the cardigan out of Sequoia's grasp as the children turned in surprise but they were too late to stop her.

'No! My treasure!' Sequoia yelled and Clover laughed, setting off at a sprint with the cardigan as her prize in the ever decreasing twilight. Chaos broke loose as the other children screamed and howled with mock fury as they chased after Clover, the tomb robber. Jake and Josh chased her down as quickly as a pair of sheepdogs.

'Clo! Go high,' shouted Ellie and Clover threw the cardigan as hard as she could over the children's heads towards Ellie before Jake and Josh reached her. There was a scramble for the cardigan but Holly was too quick and she claimed it first, dancing with savage joy at her victory.

'Death to the tomb robbers!' screamed Olivia, who was far too deeply into her role to stop at this point. A final hectic chase around the lawn had everyone breathless and tired out.

As they played, darkness crept up around them and by the time they made their way towards the blazing lights of the house, night had fallen. All that remained was to get the children to bed.

'Go and get yourself a cup of tea, I'll take it from here,' Clover said to Ellie.

'You didn't really think I was going to give them nightmares with spooky stories did you Clo?' Ellie asked.

‘I should have known better,’ said Clover with a smile. ‘I’ll be up in a bit,’ she added, ‘I’ll just make sure they really settle down before I turn out the lights.’

Clover visited her room briefly to collect a paperback and her torch while the children buzzed around brushing their teeth. It didn’t take more than fifteen minutes before they were all ready for bed.

The rest of the house was silent and Clover visited the dorm rooms for the boys and the girls to explain the rules for settling down.

‘Once we turn the lights out, no more chat, OK?’ she said. ‘I mean it, if you keep each other up talking then it always turns into a row in the end. I’ve looked after a lot of classes on trips like this and, believe me, I know.’

Josh and Jake were the only inhabitants of the boys’ dorm but she gave them the same speech anyway. They looked as if they’d managed to make peace with each other now they were separated from their respective friends.

Clover took one of the spare pillows in each room and used it to brace the doors open temporarily. She took a final pillow for herself. She found a spot in the corridor and put her pillow down to use as a cushion.

Clover said a final goodnight before putting out all the lights except for the ones in the bathrooms. In the darkness outside the dorms, Clover sat down with her back against the wall and took a deep breath. It was so good to spend time with the children. It made it easier to put up with the rest of the nonsense.

Her thoughts began to drift towards wondering how Tom was doing. His room was just a few doors away. She’d been able to avoid thinking about sneaking in to visit him while she’d been playing with the children and now she suddenly felt guilty about not going to visit him.

She peered along the ground floor corridor and tipped her head to the side. There was a sliver of deeper darkness at the tiny crack under his door. Tom was undoubtedly asleep. '*Priorities, Clover,*' she whispered to herself, '*I must think about this more clearly.*'

There was an indistinct half-whisper from inside the girl's dorm room, 'Shush!' said Clover, gently. The whispering stopped. Clover had learned from experience that if she spent the first half hour or so within earshot of the children, insisting on silence, then boredom and tiredness would generally win out and a sleepy consensus would mean that all the children got a good night's rest. Leaving them to their own devices immediately after lights-out could lead to the opposite effect with endless games of clandestine whispering and derring-do as children sneaked about trying not to get caught. If that kind of thing got started it would soon escalate and someone would have to go and sort out the trouble that would inevitably ensue.

There was silence from the boys' room; they were used to sharing with each other and had probably dropped off to sleep already.

Clover sat in the darkness, mustering the willpower to read her book by torchlight. She loved her current read. It was called, *The Secret History* by Donna Tartt and Clover had been meaning to get around to it for ages. Now that she'd finally started it, she found it completely mesmerising. However, it had been a very long day and she wasn't sure she had the energy left to read. She'd dabbled with investigating a mystery again. A dangerous game, she mused, thinking about how a murder had twisted the lives of the characters in her novel. That whole business was probably best left to the professionals.

She was about to close the children's doors and slip off to her own room when there was a soft movement on the stairs. Clover froze. Whoever it was, they were trying not to make a sound. They certainly wouldn't expect to find a teacher sitting in the middle of a corridor on a pillow. Clover carefully climbed to her feet and, shifting her weight gently on the old floorboards, made her way towards the staircase.

A ghostly figure in white seemed to float above the floor. It fluttered as it moved through the hazy darkness.

Clover snapped on her torch and the figure stumbled, turning around to face the glare of the light. It was Sophie King, wearing a loose, white nightdress and looking wild-eyed, as if she'd been caught in the midst of something criminal. She raised her hands in terrified surrender. Clover realised that Sophie couldn't see anything except the glare of the torch and pointed the beam away onto the wall to stop it from dazzling her.

'Sophie, it's only me,' whispered Clover, is everything alright?' Sophie took a deep breath and was about to reply when the door she had been creeping towards opened and light blazed out from the room inside.

Gryff stood in the doorway, initially eyeing Sophie with a predatory grin before noticing Clover in the hallway. His mood changed and he closed the door on Sophie indifferently, as if she had come to the wrong room. Sophie looked ashen as she glanced back towards Clover then at the door once more. 'This isn't what it seems,' she whispered, 'please, let me explain.'

12

Clover and Sophie both stared at each other on the dark landing. Sophie seemed unsure of what to do with her arms and she alternated between pulling the hem of her nightie down a little lower and folding her arms in front of her chest. She wasn't dressed very modestly for creeping around the building in the middle of the night, 'This *isn't* what it looks like at all,' Sophie said, pleadingly.

'What *do* you think this looks like?' asked Clover.

'As if I was sneaking into Gryff's room for a bit of fun.'

‘So it’s *not* that?’

‘No, it’s not at all. It’s *love*, true love.’

‘With Gryffin Parr?’ Clover tried to suspend her disbelief but she couldn’t hide how revolting the idea seemed. Gryff was physically very handsome by any standard but after meeting him properly Clover couldn’t imagine anyone would want to spend time with him.

Sophie read Clover’s expression. ‘You don’t understand him, that’s all. You don’t know what he’s really like.’

‘What is he really like?’ asked Clover.

‘He’s brave.’ Sophie looked away and she suddenly seemed quite girlish. She was clearly besotted with him. ‘He takes what he wants in life and he doesn’t let society’s rules tie him up in knots.’

‘So you knew each other before this weekend?’ asked Clover, puzzled over the facts.

‘We’ve known each other forever,’ said Sophie defiantly, ‘it’s as if we loved each other in another life but we’ve only just found each other in this lifetime.’

Clover shook her head, baffled by this.

‘Don’t you dare laugh at me,’ said Sophie. ‘Just because you haven’t felt this kind of love you’ve no idea how long a few months can seem. I was a completely different person before we met. I was only pretending to exist before and now I don’t have to pretend any more.’

The passion in Sophie’s voice was enough to make Clover pause. She sorted through her own feelings and realised with a start that she was envious. ‘What about Bernard?’ she asked, more gently.

‘What about him?’ Sophie retorted. ‘He’s passed out in our room, after doping himself up with drugs to sleep through the night, just like he dopes himself up with his work and his hobbies to get him through his days. He doesn’t care what I get up to.’

'You mean he knows about you and Gryff?'

'No, of course not,' said Sophie, looking at Clover as if she was stupid.

'But Neal seemed to know something,' said Clover, 'he made a very suggestive comment to Bernard about keeping an eye on you.'

'Neal didn't know anything. He was just jealous, that's all,' Sophie replied. 'If you must know, he was quite…flirtatious… with me when we first arrived. I liked it, there's no shame in that.'

'But you weren't interested because Gryffin Parr was the love of your life?' Clover asked.

'Yes, exactly,' said Sophie. 'Do you have any idea how dangerous it can be for your health if you don't follow your emotions? Feelings that go unheard can sabotage a lot more than your ability to learn. They can ruin your whole life.'

Clover started to object but found the words sticking in her throat. How much did she suppress her own emotions every day? It was part of her work to put on a happy face, it was all part of the everyday bravery of facing the class and setting a tone for the children to follow. You couldn't do your job if you were listening to your own feelings of sadness or loneliness at the same time as teaching a lesson.

'You have to be professional about things though, don't you?' said Clover.

'That's all very well but how far should we go to avoid hurting other people's feelings? Should we allow ourselves to live meaningless lives just because it might make someone else feel bad?'

Clover floundered. 'I'm not judging you,' she said. 'But I do think that you have to tell Inspector Marsh about what's going on between you and Gryff.'

'Why? You can't think that it has any bearing on the *accident*?'

‘I don’t think anyone’s absolutely certain that Neal’s death is an accident, not just yet.’

‘Please, you can’t expect us to tell Inspector Marsh about this.’

‘I can’t believe that you didn’t tell him already,’ said Clover. ‘If your…your *attachment*...to Gryff comes out without you bringing it to Marsh’s attention yourself then it might seem like you have something much bigger to hide.’

Clover looked towards Gryff’s door, suddenly wary of the man on the other side, ‘Are you absolutely certain that Gryff hasn’t got anything to do with what happened to Neal?’

‘One hundred percent!’ said Sophie, forgetting to whisper.

The door opened and Gryff looked out warily, ‘You’re going to wake up the others if you’re not careful. Are you aware of how loud you’re being out here?’ he asked in an urgent whisper.

‘Are *you* aware of the kind of trouble that you could get yourself into by keeping a secret like this from the police?’ asked Clover. Gryff waved Clover and Sophie into his room. Sophie went straight to his side but Clover didn’t move.

‘There’s no trouble here apart from the trouble that you are making, Miss Lightfoot,’ said Gryff, he’d obviously been listening to them from the other side of his door. ‘There’s certainly no need for anyone to go pouring their hearts out to Inspector Marsh. Our private lives have got nothing to do with what happened to Neal. In fact, unlike many people around here, we actually have an alibi for the night when that terrible accident took place.’

‘That’s right, we were together,’ said Sophie triumphantly.

‘I’m afraid that might not help you with Inspector Marsh,’ said Clover. ‘You both share a common motive for making sure Neal didn’t reveal anything about your relationship. There’s no two ways about it, you have to come clean and talk to the police or I’ll have to say something myself.’

Gryff glowered at her, but just then there was a heavy thump from further along the corridor.

‘What was that?’ asked Sophie clinging to Gryff. Clover pointed her torch into the darkness but there was nothing to be seen. The long corridor ahead of her had doors on each side and one of them was now wide open.

‘That was Neal’s room,’ muttered Gryff drawing back a little further into his own doorway.

‘Didn’t the police seal it up?’ asked Sophie.

‘Well if they did, it’s not sealed any more,’ said Gryff.

‘There’s someone in there,’ said Sophie, pushing her way behind Gryff and retreating into his room. Clover took a step forward. Her torch threw a bright beam ahead of her that would dazzle anyone in sight. She was aware that her hand was trembling but she was determined to investigate. She thought about calling for help but then she remembered the children sleeping downstairs with the doors braced open and the last thing she wanted was for any of them to come running. She looked back at Gryff. ‘Stay close to me,’ she whispered firmly, Gryff scowled at her but he nodded his agreement.

Clover took a few steps further down the corridor, ‘We know there’s someone in there! Come out and show yourself’ she said.

There was no sound or movement from the room. Clover took a deep breath and walked to the threshold, shining her torch into the darkness. She felt for a light switch but there was no sign of one by the door. Swann Hall was a quirky old building and hardly any of the fittings were standard.

Clover swept the room with her torch but no-one was visible. ‘I think the light switch is on the other wall, behind the door,’ she said to Gryff.

‘You’d better turn it on then, hadn’t you,’ said Gryff, keeping back near the doorway. Clover angled the torch to see if she could catch anyone hiding under the bed and then slipped quickly around the door and snapped on the light. The light strobed, blinking rapidly as it struggled to ignite.

A dark figure, swathed in black from head to toe, burst out from behind the long curtains and ran towards the door.

Clover jumped away, brandishing her torch in front of her. Gryff stumbled backward and tripped as the figure rushed towards him. He curled up in a ball and cringed as the dark shape almost trod on him as it scrambled for the door. There was no sign of who the person might be, a black hood covered their head and shoulders completely.

There was a shriek from the corridor as Sophie slammed Gryff's door closed in terror, shutting herself in his room.

'Hey! Stop!' Clover shouted after the figure in black as Gryff huddled on the floor. She leaped over him and stumbled to the door. She shone her torch down the long corridor but there was nothing to see. Clover clutched at her heart to try to stop it from beating so wildly in her chest and she slumped back against the door frame, as she took in the wreckage of Neal's room.

Someone had scattered Neal's papers across the desk and they were spilled all over the floor. The bedclothes were heaped on top of the bed and an empty suitcase lay open on top of them. Gryff was uncurling from his position on the floor but he was still on his knees. She could hear the sounds of others in the rooms along the corridors getting out of bed to investigate.

Mr Fish was the first to open his door and he looked very surprised to see Clover standing in the corridor with a torch, 'What's going on Clover?' he asked.

Julie Giroux peered out from her room too, closely followed by Zuzie, Jeremy Billingham and Jacqui Scarfe. The only doors that stayed closed were the door to Gryff's room, where Sophie was still hiding, and the door to Sophie and Bernard's room, presumably because Bernard was still asleep, knocked out by his sleeping pills.

'Someone's been in Neal's room searching for something,' Clover announced as Ellie appeared in her pyjamas at the far end of the corridor. Ellie looked alarmed but the person in black clearly hadn't run up the short flight of stairs towards her. There hadn't been time for them to descend via the main staircase either. Could one of the consultants have been the figure in the black cloak? Clover wasn't sure.

'Go back into your rooms and close your doors,' she instructed them. Ellie and I will sleep downstairs with the children tonight but first, I'll put in a call to Inspector Marsh. Don't *any* of you come downstairs until the police get here!'

Jeremy Billingham looked as if he was about to speak but Clover wasn't about to have a discussion when it came to the children's safety.

'Back in your room!' she said, pointing at him fiercely. Mr Billingham turned to Simon Fish for support but Simon had already closed his door behind him.

'Bring a duvet,' Clover said to Ellie, and we'll camp out downstairs until the police get here.

Clover looked back at Gryff, who was on his feet once more and recovering himself. He had undoubtedly been terrified when the thief had jumped out at them.

'Who was that?' asked Clover.

Gryff straightened himself up, 'I couldn't tell,' he said. 'But it certainly wasn't me or Sophie. So, who are you going to point the finger at next, Miss Lightfoot?'

13

It wasn't until after sunrise that Clover knocked on Tom's door and peeped inside. Tom was in bed but he looked less pale and drawn. Clover beamed, 'I wasn't sure if you were awake or not,' she said. How are you feeling?'

‘Much better, thanks,’ said Tom, sitting up in bed. ‘You look a bit tired yourself though,’ he said. ‘What have you been up to?’

‘Me and Ellie spent the night in the corridor, camping outside the children’s dorm rooms. I’m not sure if it was strictly necessary but I was a bit rattled.’

Tom looked wide awake suddenly, ‘Why, what happened?’

‘There was an incident in the night. Someone broke into Neal’s room. I happened to walk in on the thief while they were in the act but they managed to slip away somehow.’

‘Are you alright?’ Tom took her hand immediately, giving it a squeeze.

‘Mostly. I’m a bit shaken up but nothing more than that.’

‘You didn’t see who it was?’

‘No, the lights were flickering and the person had a black hood covering their head. They definitely didn’t want to be recognised. Anyway, the police are back now and they’re on the case.’

‘What’s going on in this place?’ Tom shook his head, dropping back onto his pillows. He seemed completely exhausted again by the thought of trying to puzzle it out.

Clover squeezed his hand in return, ‘It’s all very strange. I was trying to leave things to the police...’ Tom gave her a knowing grin and she paused, changing her story. ‘Alright, I was trying to make sure I didn’t get in the police’s way while I did a little bit of investigating of my own, but Inspector Marsh warned me off. Now I think I should have kept going.’

‘Why’s that?’

‘From the way he’s been interviewing people, Inspector Marsh seems to believe that Neal was killed because someone lost their temper with him. Neal certainly had a talent for infuriating people but I’m not sure that’s why he died.’

‘What makes you think that?’

‘I’ve been wondering why someone would want to search Neal’s room. Neal had a manuscript linked to his *Mind-Robics* programme. It didn’t seem particularly impressive to me but it was apparently very exclusive and there were all kinds of rules about paying for a licence just to take a look at it. I wondered if someone might be interested in a secret like that.’

‘Do you think that someone might have stolen the manuscript?’ asked Tom.

‘I don’t know, but Neal’s papers were a complete mess once the thief had left. Maybe Inspector Marsh will tell us if anything was taken. He’s up there with his constables looking at the evidence now.’

‘I bet you have a theory about who did it, don’t you?’ said Tom.

Clover grimaced, ‘Actually, I don’t. I’ve been running through a list of possible suspects and I can’t see that any of them had a motive for murder. The police were interested in Jacqui Scarfe because she had a public argument with Neal. But I've read her books and I know how she thinks. I don’t believe for a minute that she’s capable of murder.’

Clover counted off the people on her fingers. ‘Bernard King was an unknown quantity until I found out how fragile he really is so I really don’t think he’s got anything to do with it.

The mystery of Zuzie Zuleika's little chats with Neal turned out to be nothing more than discussions about promoting this weekend’s event.’

Clover continued, ‘Gryffin Parr and Sophie King seem to… *know each other*…rather well but they must be innocent because they were with me when I stumbled on the person in black breaking into Neal’s room.’

Clover kept tallying the list of consultants, ‘Julie Giroux is a very respectable journalist and I can’t imagine any reason in the world why she’d get involved in something as desperate as this. I know it’s not you, Ellie, me or Mr Fish,’ she counted off all the fingers of her second hand as she spoke.

‘Who else is there?’ asked Tom,

‘I’m not at all sure about Jeremy Billingham,’ said Clover. ‘He did get us invited to this weekend in the first place.’

Tom shook his head, ‘That’s probably just a coincidence. We’ve brought the Year 6 children here for years. I asked Jeremy to help organise the payment for the children’s visit. He is Deputy Head, after all. I’m sure that’s the only reason he came across this consultants’ weekend event and decided to inflict it on us too.’

‘That makes sense.’ Clover sighed thoughtfully. ‘This is so frustrating. I feel like I’m missing something but I can’t imagine what.’

‘Talk to the police if you get any more ideas,’ Tom suggested. ‘That’s what they’re there for. Whatever’s going on here, it’s their responsibility not yours, Miss Lightfoot.’

Clover smiled, ‘I know but you know how it is, sometimes I can’t resist.’ She met his eyes, seriously.

He nodded, smiling gently. ‘I understand,’ he said. ‘So how are the children doing?’

‘They’re fine, they’re still asleep. They were due to go home today anyway so I presume Mr Fish won’t have any trouble reaching their parents this time. And there are only six of them left so I’m sure it won’t be difficult to look after them.’

‘I’ll come and help,’ offered Tom.

‘Oh no you won’t. I’ll bring you some breakfast in bed but I don’t think you’re up to helping with anything right now.’

‘I should get up. I’m feeling much better and it’s not like I’ll be doing any kayaking or anything.’

‘I said no. Stay!’ She put her hand on his chest and he lay still. Clover looked away shyly, ‘I don’t think there’s going to be any more kayaking here anyway. From the sound of things, this incident might be enough to ruin Swann Hall once and for all.’

Inspector Marsh, Constable Gregory and several uniformed officers had arrived before dawn and they went straight upstairs to investigate Neal's room. Marsh looked far from pleased about being back at Swann Hall at such an early hour.

The children woke slowly, unaware of what had taken place during the night. They were much quieter than they had been when the whole class was present and they set about using the bathrooms, getting dressed and chatting happily as if everything was quite normal. Clover was cheered by that.

It seemed as if a lengthy investigation process was taking place upstairs. Constable Gregory quietly came to tell Clover that everything was in hand and that she should concentrate on getting the children home. He passed on the list of contact details that Mr Fish had been working on.

'Have you got any new leads?' Clover asked Constable Gregory as he started back towards the stairs.

'Never you mind, Miss,' replied Gregory but he smiled as if to confirm that there had been some new developments. Clover considered following him to try to find out what was going on. It was frustrating to be in the dark about what Marsh was up to, but there really wasn't anything she could do, especially as he had made it so clear that her skills as a sleuth were not required.

While Clover supervised breakfast, Ellie took over with the phone calls. By now, Tony had arrived. He appeared to be the only employee of Swann Hall. He seemed as sullen as usual and he wore headphones as he poured cereals out from their Tupperware containers, ignoring as much of the activity that took place around him as he could.

Clover felt a sense of despondency as she ladled out a bowl of Rice Crispies. The thought of Swann Hall closing forever seemed to be a strong possibility. She wasn't particularly attached to the place but she could see what an impact visiting the Hall had made on Ellie and Zuzie when they were young. She felt moved to try to chat to Tony as he refilled the milk jug.

‘Has Lord Swann talked to you about what’s going on around here?’ she asked.

Tony slipped off his headphones and let them dangle around his neck. His thick tangled hair was once again contained in a hairnet. Tony shrugged, ‘Lord Swann doesn’t tell me anything, he never has. But he’s pretty good at complaining when something doesn’t happen the way he wants it to.’

‘I bet,’ said Clover with a sympathetic smile. ‘I hear that you’re not getting so many visitors these days,’ she said.

‘Nope, I expect you’ll be the last of them,’ said Tony, indifferently.

Clover was puzzled, ‘You don’t sound very upset.’

‘It’s been a long time coming, so it’s no surprise. Lord Swann has me do the weekly shopping and last week he told me not to bother again. I don’t expect he’ll be needing my help if there’s nobody here, so I reckon that’s about it for me here.’

‘He told you this last week?’ asked Clover.

‘Yeah. I suppose he knew he didn’t have any other bookings right after you.’

‘Is it normal for you to stop work when there’s no bookings then?’

‘Yeah, but usually if that happens, he’ll let me know when we’re going to start up again. This time he hasn’t told me a thing. ‘Why, is it important?’

‘Probably not,’ said Clover, ‘Lord Swann doesn’t strike me as the most organised individual I’ve ever met. If it wasn’t for you I don’t think he could keep this place going at all,’ Tony allowed himself a rare smile at this.

‘It’s hard to get good help around here. There are no villages for miles. Legend has it that nobody wanted to build their houses this close to Hatton Hoo.’ He glanced out the windows of the dining hall towards the distant hill. ‘Of course, the jokes on them now because of the visitor centre and all that.’

‘What?’ asked Clover. ‘What kind of visitor centre?’

‘A big one,’ said Tony. ‘Got the money from the European Union, the papers said, they’re going to build it some time next year.’

‘Where are they going to build this visitor centre?’ asked Clover.

‘Hasn’t been decided, it’s a big council ding-dong but someone’s going to get rich off it. The only thing for certain is that it’s going to be someone who’s already rolling in it.’

‘Will having a new visitor centre bring more people to Swann Hall too?’ asked Clover.

Tony shrugged, ‘Can’t hurt I suppose,’ he said. ‘But you’d have to ask Lord Swann about that.’

‘I might just do that,’ said Clover. ‘Oh and just one more thing, you said that there’s no villages for miles, does that mean you stay here overnight?’

‘No chance! I’m a cyclist so I cycle here and back every day as part of my schedule. That’s why I always eat at home and spend the evenings working with my dad, I’m in training.’ A note of determination had entered Tony’s voice for the first time.

‘What are you in training for?’ asked Clover

‘The Sydney Olympics in 2000.’

‘But that’s four years from now!’

‘That’s what it takes,’ he said. ‘I missed out on going to Atlanta this year but I’ll make myself another chance.’

‘I’m sure you will,’ said Clover. Tony’s routine was something that Inspector Marsh could easily check up on. Now that Clover understood what was behind his foul mood, it seemed far less likely to have anything to do with foul play.

As it happened, Clover didn’t have time to do anything else before she saw Ellie coming down the corridor, her face set.

‘What’s the matter?’ asked Clover.

'It sounds like there was some confusion when the coach got back to the school yesterday. It didn't help that Mr Fish hadn't told any of the parents the real reason that the trip was cut short. So it seems like they were trying to guess and making up reasons of their own.'

'Oh dear, what were they saying?'

'All kinds of things from unlikely problems with the water supply to escaped wild animals from nearby zoos.'

'There really aren't any nearby zoos,' said Clover.

'Well maybe that's something that Mr Fish should have thought about mentioning when he called them all up and started being evasive.'

'What *did* he say, exactly?'

'As little as he possibly could, I think, which only made the parents imagine it was something really horrific.'

'Wonderful,' said Clover sarcastically.

'Oh that's not the best part,' said Ellie. 'Sandy Delaney and Bettina Williams found out about it from the other parents and they're driving out here this morning to collect their own children and take the others home too.'

Clover shuddered. Sandy Delaney was Olivia's mum and also the Chair of the school's Board of Governors. She had a fearsome reputation and if she was on her way out to Swann Hall then she wasn't about to go home again without finding out every detail of everything that had gone on. At least Bettina Williams would be there too. She was Jake and Josh's mum and she also happened to be the head of the Parent Teacher Association. Bettina was infinitely sensible, far less dramatic and she, at least, could be relied upon to grasp the practicalities of the situation.

'How did you find out that they're on their way?' Clover asked.

'I got through to Mr Delaney and he sounded a bit nervous. Sandy must have been furious when she left.'

'That's what happens when parents aren't told what's happening to their children,' said Clover. 'You didn't happen to check if the other parents have given their consent for Sandy and Bettina to collect their children did you?'

'They know the drill,' said Ellie, 'I checked just in case and it's all fine.'

'Well done. Do you have any idea what time they'll arrive?'

'My guess is that they won't get here for at least three hours. I got the impression they'd just set off.'

'That's a relief. I hope, for Mr Fish's sake, that things will have calmed down by then.'

'What are we going to do with the children for the next three hours?' asked Ellie.

'I've got some ideas,' said Clover. 'I saw some things in the classroom that we might be able to use. Can you make sure the children get a good breakfast and I'll see what I can rustle up.'

Ellie went to see to the children and Clover made her way to the empty classroom at the far end of the corridor. In the classroom she found the children's sketchbooks and looked through to see what they'd already done. There were lots of pencil drawings of the outside of the house and some maps of the area. On other pages they'd drawn diagrams of the differences between voles and mice. There were also pages where they'd sketched *mini beasts*; beetles and worms that they'd found in soil samples. Clover couldn't help but smile when she thought about the fun the children must have had.

Looking around for other possibilities, she investigated the big stainless steel sink. There were about ten paintbrushes there, in various states of repair and four battle-scarred plastic paint pallets, thickly encrusted with layers of dried-on, ready-mixed paint that must have been squirted from the tubes lying in the tray nearby. There was plenty of paint left as long as you liked bright red, deep purple, black or orange but there wasn't any green or blue. This probably wasn't surprising, given that the children who'd last used these paints would have been painting the lush colours of the landscape.

Clover investigated further. At the back of the deep, paint-spattered wooden shelves under the sink Clover found two large, sealed tubs of powder paint, covered in dust. There were only two colours but Clover beamed with satisfaction when she saw what they were.

She gathered up a box of supplies, only pausing to fill up a big, green, plastic watering-can from the sink to provide a water source. Now she had everything she needed.

14

The mid-morning sun blazed down on the lawn, warming the five stone steps that led down from the driveway onto the grass. Ellie had made sure that the children had all eaten a good breakfast and by the time Clover came to find them, they had repacked their belongings ready to leave as soon as their parents arrived.

From the lawn, Clover caught a glimpse of Zuzie and Julie through the French windows of the dining hall. Inspector Marsh had been keeping the guests in their rooms while he'd been taking more statements but it looked as if they had finally been allowed downstairs for breakfast.

Inspector Marsh was clearly taking the events of the previous evening extremely seriously. Clover suspected that he might also be paying everyone back for the inconvenience of being awakened in the early hours of the morning.

Clover put the strange business of what was going on inside the house to the back of her mind. It was certainly far easier to do that when she had a group of children to work with. She settled herself down, cross-legged, on the grass and the children sat watching from the steps.

'I've got everything we need to do some landscape painting but first of all I need to teach you a little practice exercise,' said Clover. She took a sheet of paper and laid it on the grass in front of her. Then she quickly popped open the lids of the two powder-paint containers and showed the colours to the children. They were vivid yellow and bright blue. 'Even if we only had these two colours we'd have everything we need to make dozens of different shades of green,' she said.

She poured a beaker of water from the watering-can as she began her demonstration, 'Some people like tubes of ready-mixed paints because they think it takes some of the work out of painting, but I much prefer using powder-paints because you can mix all the colours that you need so much more easily.'

The children watched quietly as Clover's brush went from the water to the paint and then to the pallet. As she repeated the sequence of movements, Clover said, 'I made up a little rhyme for this bit, to help me remember the order.'

'*Take a dip,*' she dabbed her brush into the water and caught the drip on the lip of the beaker, '*get a bit,*' she continued, touching the damp brush to the brightly coloured paint, taking care not to scoop up too much powder. 'Then, *thicken it,*' she said as she painted the deep blue colour onto her pallet. She repeated the sequence of dipping her brush, catching the excess water and then gathering more paint and mixing it. Soon she had a perfectly mixed circle of smooth, blue paint that was no bigger than a ten pence piece.

Clover glanced up at the children's faces as they watched her expectantly.

'We're going to start with blue and then mix in yellow so we can make as many different shades of green as we can,' she said. She repeated the same sequence of dipping her brush into the water, the paint and then the mixing pallet but this time she used the yellow paint instead of the blue.

The colour of the paint in her pallet changed into a deep, sea green. Clover carefully painted a circle of this new colour around the pure blue dot at the centre of her paper. As the paint dried, the change in colour became even more apparent.

Clover repeated the process to mix another dab of yellow into her dark green colour. Then she painted a second circle surrounding the first. This time the green was a shade brighter as the yellow started to lighten it.

'So, first of all, I'd like everyone to paint a pattern like this that shows how you mix colours to change them gradually. You could start with a dot and paint circles of colours around it or choose another pattern that shows the colours side by side. After you've had a go at that then we can all try painting a landscape.'

Julie Giroux emerged from the house, nursing a cup of tea. She took a breath of fresh air and smiled in the direction of the children.

'Oh, tea!' whispered Ellie enviously. 'Want some?'

'Let me get you a cup, Ellie, you supervised all the packing.'

It was a pleasure to do something for Ellie. Clover also considered going to offer Tom a cup of tea too but he was probably still asleep; he'd seemed pretty wiped out after their talk.

Jacqui Scarfe and Sophie King were still in the dining room, both looking rather exhausted. Inspector Marsh had undoubtedly been exacting in his interrogations this morning as he tried to discover who had ransacked Neal's room.

Clover poured out two cups of tea and returned to the children. They were quietly focused on their work and Ellie had taken up Clover's demonstration painting to continue it herself.

Clover let her curiosity get the better of her again and wandered across the lawn to talk to Julie Giroux.

'Are you alright?' Clover asked. 'It's been the strangest weekend, hasn't it?'

'I'll say,' said Julie, peering meditatively into her tea.

‘Last night was so scary. Did you manage to sleep much?’

‘Not really,’ said Julie.

‘Me neither,’ smiled Clover. ‘Do you know what’s happening upstairs?’

‘They’re searching everyone’s rooms and their belongings. I believe they’re looking for Mr Skinner’s *Mind-Robics* manuscript as it appears to have gone missing from his room.’

‘It sounds like quite a few people were interested in Neal’s work,’ said Clover.

‘Yes, I was one of them.’ Julie shook her head, ‘I’d heard of similar things going around before but I’d been too slow to investigate them. This seemed like the perfect opportunity to be the first to find out about some new research.’

Clover bit her lip, ‘I have to confess, from what I heard of Neal’s work I didn’t find it especially convincing.’

Julie laughed lightly, ‘Well you have good instincts and, speaking confidentially, I absolutely agree with you. The more I looked into *Mind-Robics* the less convinced I became. It was a very interesting story though and it’s my job to find good stories. Too bad it’s all going to be overshadowed by this mess. It will be all I can do to save my own reputation. I can’t really afford to be tangled up in something like this.’

‘I don’t see how you can be blamed for anything,’ said Clover. ‘All you did was attend the same conference as Neal. That hardly qualifies as being tangled up in something.’

Clover paused. She was suddenly distracted by a memory from the night before. In her mind’s eye, she could see the strobing glare of the strip light in Neal’s room. There, amongst the papers scattered across Neal’s desk, she remembered seeing the bright yellow folder that Julie had been carrying the day before. Julie’s folder was lying open on Neal’s desk and it was empty. Clover thought for a moment but she couldn’t imagine how it had ended up there.

‘You didn’t happen to give Neal your yellow folder, did you?’ Clover asked.

‘My folder, no, certainly not,’ said Julie but as she spoke, Clover noticed that her teacup shook slightly in her hand.

‘It’s just that I thought I saw it in Neal’s room.’

‘My folder? You must have been mistaken,’ said Julie moving to hold her teacup with both hands to steady it.

‘I don’t think so,’ said Clover, ‘it was a very distinctive colour. I saw you with it on Friday night, Gryff used it in his demonstration but he gave it back to you right away afterwards.’

‘Oh, that is very strange. Perhaps Neal borrowed it for some reason?’ said Julie, uncertainly. Her shaking hands were now causing the tea to reach the lip of the cup, threatening to spill over her fingers.

‘If Neal was pilfering things and taking them to his room then that could be important information for Inspector Marsh’s investigation,’ said Clover carefully. ‘We should make sure he has all the facts.’

‘No! Don’t, please, it will only confuse matters,’ said Julie, clasping her teacup so tightly that her fingers started to go white.

‘Why?’ asked Clover. ‘What’s going on?’

Julie sighed. ‘I can explain everything but I was rather hoping that I wouldn’t have to. It’s a little embarrassing, professionally speaking. I was the one who gave you a fright in Neal’s room last night.’

Clover was dumbfounded, ‘You? You were the one hiding behind the curtains?’ She looked back towards the house and considered rushing off to tell Inspector Marsh at once.

‘Wait, please, let me explain,’ said Julie, so mildly that Clover stopped to listen. ‘I was contacted by Neal about this weekend’s event and I was actually very impressed. He told me that both Gryffin Parr and Jacqui Scarfe were likely to attend and he had my interest right away. Then he started talking to me about *Mind-Robics*.’ Julie shook her head again, ’I got greedy. My job is to report on new trends in education and this could have been an exclusive. You have to understand that I had good reason to believe several rival publishing organisations were interested. So I decided I had to move quickly.'

'What did you do?' asked Clover.

'I prepared a contract that I was hoping Mr Skinner might sign. The contract offered quite a large sum of money to Neal if he would agree to serialise some writing on *Mind-Robics* for my newspaper. I presented him with a copy of the contract on Friday night.'

'Just before he died,' Clover said, thinking it through. 'So there was a lucrative contract, inside your yellow folder, in Neal's room when the police first came. Why didn't you talk to the police about it at that point?'

'I didn't imagine that the police would have any reason to go through Neal's papers at that point. But last night I just wanted to get my contract back.'

'So that's why you broke into Neal's room?'

'It wasn't like that,' said Julie, 'I was very shocked by what happened to Neal. I couldn't sleep. I was restless and needed to go to the bathroom at the end of the hall. That's when I saw that the room's seal was broken. I went to look and saw that the room had been already searched and the place was a mess.'

'So you're telling me that someone broke into the room before you even got there?'

'Exactly, I was just passing but when I saw the folder with my contract offer right in the middle of that mess, I took the opportunity to take it back. That's all I did. But when I heard someone on the stairs, I knew I couldn't get back to my room without being seen so I turned out the lights and tried to hide until you'd gone. But when you came in to investigate I panicked.'

'Just passing?' asked Clover. 'The person I encountered was dressed in black from head to toe.'

Julie attempted a casual shrug. 'I like black and I happened to be wearing my robe when I realised I was trapped. I improvised. You have to believe me, I simply sought to recover a document that belonged to me, to which I was a co-signatory. There's was nothing more to it than that except that it makes me look rather suspicious, of course. Would it really be so bad if I edited myself out of this little conundrum?'

'If only it were that simple,' replied Clover. 'You must tell Inspector Marsh what you did and what your reasons were or he's going to keep on looking in the wrong places for the wrong thing.'

'Can you be so sure of that, Miss Lightfoot? Remember, someone else broke into that room before I happened by and someone took the *Mind-Robics* manuscript. It certainly wasn't me. But Inspector Marsh is looking for the manuscript right now and I think that's probably the best clue to the identity of Neal's killer.'

Clover wavered, unsure of what to do next. She hadn't meant to quiz Julie quite so thoroughly but surely it was wrong to ignore evidence when it was revealed to her?

The decision was taken out of her hands, however, as Constable Gregory approached them from the other side of the lawn.

'Could you come with me please, Miss Giroux?' he asked stiffly.

'Why, of course, Constable,' replied Julie handing Clover her teacup. 'Though I don't know what more you could possibly ask me that I haven't given an answer to already.'

'My apologies, Madam, but in a case like this, we have to be certain that we've covered everything.'

'Constable Gregory,' said Clover. 'Will Inspector Marsh be free to talk to me at some point today?'

'I think he's ruled you out already, Miss. We're very sorry for any inconvenience we've caused.'

'I'm not seeking an apology,' said Clover, 'I'm requesting a further interview with the Inspector.' She glanced at Julie,

‘Later on, of course, I’m quite certain he’s going to be very busy in the next hour or two.’

Julie glared at Clover, taking her meaning. If Julie didn’t tell Inspector Marsh the whole truth then Clover would see to it that he would learn about her actions. In just a few minutes Clover had found out a great deal more than Julie had wanted to admit.

‘You are most...unusual, Miss Lightfoot,’ said Julie unable to keep the irritation from her voice.

15

‘What was all that about?’ asked Ellie as Clover returned to the group of children, who were still painting.

‘Nothing, much. It’s just that when something shocking happens it seems to reveal who everyone really is and what they’re really up to.’

‘Clo, are you OK?’ asked Ellie gently. ‘You don’t have to solve anything, you know. The police are on the case and it’s their job to deal with all of the fallout from this.’

‘I’m honestly trying to keep out of it,’ said Clover. ‘It’s just that I seem to be some kind of evidence-magnet, that’s all.’

‘Well, try to put that magnet away,’ said Ellie, with a grin.

Sequoia looked up. She had been listening intently to their conversation and she was obviously curious but she didn’t ask about what was happening.

‘That’s beautiful,’ said Clover, smiling at Sequoia. She had completed her colour mixing quickly and had begun a painting of the trees in the distance. ‘You’ve got such a talent for this.’

‘I practice a lot,’ said Sequoia, ‘we do a lot of painting at home.’

‘You probably didn’t need the lesson in colour mixing did you?’ asked Clover.

'Oh, I don't know,' said Sequoia, reasonably, 'I mix colours all the time but I've never tried to find so many shades in between yellow and blue.' She turned the page of her art book to show Clover the pattern she'd created. The page was filled with rippling lines painted with the finest gradations of tone between them. 'It's definitely given me some ideas for the colours I want to use in the landscape.'

Clover felt genuine admiration for Sequoia. The girl loved to learn and she could find the good in every situation. Over the years, Clover had learned far more from working with the children than she could ever have taught them.

Sequoia flicked back to her landscape which was developing rapidly as she layered colours over each other with an experienced eye. The best thing that Clover could do when she worked with children who exceeded her own talents was to set up activities that gave them a lot of scope to explore and learn for themselves.

'Any advice for the rest of us?' Clover asked Sequoia.

'Just keep trying to paint what you really see in front of you, not what you expect to see,' said Sequoia, 'that's what I try to do, anyway.'

Josh and Jake were sitting close together, their shoulders touching as they leaned on each other. The twins' sometimes fraught relationship seemed to have healed itself amid the strangeness of the last two days. Tom would be pleased, Clover reflected. Sometimes the children took leaps forward academically or socially in completely unexpected ways and despite the disruptions during their trip, the twins had definitely grown from the experience.

Ellie and Clover continued to watch Sequoia as she expertly picked out the greenery that bordered the Lodge. The building was almost as large as the main house and although it may have originally been the servants' quarters, it had obviously served as a comfortable private home to Lord Swann for a long time.

‘It’s a good thing we didn’t try to paint the Lodge until today,’ said Sequoia, ‘otherwise we’d have had to paint it with all those vans parked in front of it.’

‘Vans?’ asked Clover, exchanging glances with Ellie. ‘What kind of vans?’

‘Grey ones,’ said Sequoia with a shrug. ‘There were workmen sitting on the lawn when we were supposed to have a playtime but Mr Flint said we should let them eat their sandwiches in peace.’

‘What were the workmen doing?’ asked Clover but Sequoia looked blank. Clover stood up and peered at the Lodge.

‘Leave it, Clo’ said Ellie mildly.

‘I’m just going to stretch my legs,’ said Clover. Ellie sniggered.

‘What?’ Clover asked.

‘Go on then, go and have a look, we’re fine here.’

‘I’m just interested.’

‘Better watch out, evidence-magnet,’ said Ellie.

‘Nothing’s going to happen. Besides, from here you can watch me the whole time,’ said Clover, setting off across the lawn towards the Lodge.

The garden of the Lodge was immaculately maintained compared with the rest of the grounds. The grasses had been cropped back just far enough to keep the paths clear from the lawn to the lake. Clover walked slowly towards the heavy, wooden front door, admiring the half-timbered building and the manicured vines that crept up the walls.

Catching glimpses of the interior, Clover could see an enormous fireplace with a rustic stone hearth. The walls of the room were decorated with gorgeous wallpaper that shone with golden highlights in the sunlight. Everything looked completely authentic and extremely luxurious in comparison with the shabbiness of Swann Hall. If money was being spent anywhere, it was being spent on the Lodge.

That was when she noticed that the front door of the Lodge had been left half open. She looked closer and in the deep shadows inside the doorway she saw the unmistakeable shape of a pair of feet, the sole of one shoe clearly visible.

Clover gasped and her heart raced. She ran the last few steps to fling the front door open and see who it was, only to find it was nobody at all.

What had looked like the feet of a second victim was only an empty pair of indoor slippers that were lying at a deceptive angle where they'd been discarded, just inside the lobby of the Lodge. There was a mat by the door with flakes of dried mud on the flagstones beneath it and she suspected that whoever had left the slippers behind had probably replaced them with a pair of walking boots before heading out.

Clover imagined Lord Swann, overtaken with a rush of enthusiasm, only remembering to change out of his slippers at the last minute. It was dark inside and there didn't seem to be a light switch on the wall. Still full of adrenaline, Clover walked through the lobby into a large, open hallway.

The hallway was almost completely empty, any furniture that had once been there having been removed. A plastic telephone with an old-style, round dial sat on the plain, vermilion carpet between four small, circular marks. The marks must surely have been left by the feet of a small table that had been standing there for some time. The carpet hadn't been vacuumed and the ghostly shapes of other missing pieces of furniture were marked out in a slightly brighter shade of crimson where the carpet had been protected from the gathering dust.

So Lord Swann was actually in the process of moving out? Clover guessed that the vans that Sequoia had mentioned belonged to removal men. She knew from her talk with Tony that Lord Swann wasn't expecting more visiting parties of children any time soon but now it seemed that he might have intended to move out of Swann Hall too.

'Hello!' Clover called out into the empty house. She didn't expect to receive an answer and, sure enough, she was met by silence. Walking further down the hallway, she looked into the first room to her right. It had also been emptied of furniture. Cables sprouted from the wall in an empty corner where a TV might once have stood.

Clover walked back towards the front door. This time she noticed a small pile of leaflets and papers that had been placed underneath the phone.

She crouched down to look closer. She didn't want to be nosy but even without touching them she could see that there were several large certificates with the word *insurance* printed in large letters in the titles.

On top of the insurance certificates someone had scribbled a date on one of the leaflets. The date was for the following weekend and the leaflet was for *Warringdon Abattoir and Horse Slaughter Services*.

Clover felt an icy dread grip her chest as she thought of Starbuck and Stubb, the two ponies whom the children had taken out riding the day before.

The front door slammed and Clover jumped. Lord Swann walked briskly into the hallway before Clover could get to her feet.

'Hello there. What's all this?' he said with amusement as he saw Clover by the papers.

'I'm sorry, but the door was open and for a moment I thought something awful might have happened,' said Clover awkwardly.

'As you can see, that is not the case,' said Lord Swann. 'And have you found my private legal documents to be in order, young lady?'

‘I’m sorry,’ said Clover, ‘I didn’t mean to look, I was just curious. Though I must admit I’m surprised. It looks like you’re selling Swann Hall and getting an insurance payout to keep it going at the same time,’ said Clover.

‘Well, young lady. It seems I must explain to you that this is precisely how things are supposed to work. I did indeed acquire some rather extensive insurance policies in order to help me keep my business going in the event of a tragic accident like the one we’re currently facing. Granted, it seems that the timing of this unfortunate death will result in a fortuitous insurance payment to me just at the point that I will have no need of it. The fact that I happen to be closing my business and selling Swann Hall at the same time is merely happen stance.’

‘What does Inspector Marsh have to say about that?’ Clover asked, her voice sounding rather more bold than she felt. ‘He might see a large insurance payout as a motive for all kinds of things.’

‘Marsh? Oh no, he’s already very well aware of all the facts,’ said Lord Swann with a laugh. ‘As I said, everything is perfectly fine and above board. A bit of circumstantial evidence doesn’t worry me at all. Why, if I’d had anything to do with murdering Neal Skinner, don’t you think I would have at least bothered to organise an alibi for myself.’ Clover didn’t know what to say to that. Lord Swann seemed entirely confident that his behaviour was well within the law and she felt out of her depth.

‘But you’re going to sell Starbuck and Stubb to a … a *horse slaughterer*! Surely you don’t need to do that, there are charities who would look after them for free.’

‘Oh my dear girl,’ said Lord Swann, ‘I know that you city folk don’t understand this kind of thing, but this is what one does with horses when one can no longer maintain them. There’s nothing out of the ordinary about it whatsoever. In fact, I think you’ll find that I’d be in far bigger trouble for keeping those poor beasts alive in even slightly inadequate conditions.

Having them quickly and humanely dispatched for their meat is absolutely within my rights as the owner.'

'I understand that it's legal. But it can't possibly be right,' said Clover desperately.

'It is truly fascinating to me,' said Lord Swann, 'that so many seemingly reasonable people think that way about so many perfectly natural things. I presume that you eat meat? Where do you think it comes from?'

'I…I should get back to the children,' said Clover, feeling a mixture of horror and repulsion towards Lord Swann. The things that had come to light were unpleasant but there really wasn't anything incriminating.

'Yes, my dear. You get back to that and leave me to my perfectly legal personal business.'

As Clover opened the door to go, she could see Inspector Marsh and Constable Gregory heading across the lawn towards them. Lord Swann gulped. 'Um...ah...I wonder if you might excuse me, my dear,' he said, pushing Clover lightly through the door and shutting it behind her.

Clover saw Constable Gregory breaking into a run as she stood outside, feeling perplexed.

'I'll watch the front. Go and see if he's left by the back door,' Marsh called to Gregory as the young constable ran ahead of him, veering off to run at full speed down the path by the side of the house, his feet pounding on the flagstones.

'Inspector Marsh,' Clover gasped as the policeman approached. 'What's going on?'

Marsh didn't even glance at Clover as he examined each of the windows at the front of the Lodge. 'I'll need to ask you to go back to the main house, Miss Lightfoot,' said Marsh. 'We've been quietly trying to keep the whole lot of you away from Lord Swann this entire time.'

Clover looked at him, confounded. 'Certainly not, I'm not moving until you tell me exactly what's going on here.'

To her surprise, rather than dismissing her, Marsh addressed Clover directly. 'You've all been conned, Miss Lightfoot. You, your headteacher, the other consultants, the lot of you.' He let out a grim laugh. 'There was no such person as Neal Skinner. I've just had confirmation that the dead man who was posing as Mr Skinner was actually, a well known con man with a record as long as your arm. Neal was just one of his many aliases.'

Clover was stunned, 'What?' she managed.

Marsh continued, 'Yes Miss Lightfoot, it seems that the deceased individual known as Mr Skinner was colluding with Lord Swann to take you all for a ride.'

Clover's head spun. It had never occurred to her that Neal might not have been a real consultant. It was true that she hadn't ever heard of him or read anything by him and she realised that the respect that had been paid to him by the other educational consultants was the only standard of proof that was generally required.

'His usual con was impersonation and false claims for injury insurance,' continued Marsh. 'The individual in question had a habit of staging minor accidents for himself that resulted in large payouts to the owner of the premises to cover damages. Mr Skinner himself, using whatever name was convenient, would also pocket a tidy sum for his trouble. I'm sure that is what he and Lord Swann planned to do here all along. A minor accident, with some credible witnesses confirming Neal's identity. A small deception and a large insurance payout to split between them.'

'So what happened?' asked Clover.

'I believe that Lord Swann got greedy. Perhaps he didn't fancy having a partner in crime after all. They had always planned to stage an accident. Neal knew how to pretend that he'd injured his neck or his back. All Lord Swann had to do was ensure that the accident they had planned to fake turned into something very real and ultimately, something fatal. Under the terms of his insurance arrangements he would get a far bigger payout and he wouldn't have to split it with anyone.'

The sounds of Constable Gregory banging on the back door could be heard from the front of house, 'Come on out please, Lord Swann!' called Marsh.

'But what tipped you off?' asked Clover.

Marsh looked at her as if she was hopelessly naive, 'Miss Lightfoot, I believe that you are under the illusion that this is a cheap detective story set in the 1930s. This is 1996. Since his death, we've been using the most up-to-date methods to compile evidence about the man who identified himself as Neal Skinner. Fingerprints, credit card records...we store these electronically now. Some of the evidence was even more obvious. Lord Swann's plans to sell up were hardly a well kept secret and it's clear that the whole place was being run into the ground. Lord Swann's appetite for cash is so large that it's practically visible from space.'

'If you knew who'd done it, why didn't you act sooner?' asked Clover.

'We were acting, we were simply biding our time and building our case. We were also keeping an eye out for accomplices. But rest assured, he never had the slightest chance of getting away with this. We are professional investigators Miss Lightfoot, did you actually think that you could solve this murder as if it were a parlour game?' Clover blanched. She didn't have an answer to that. 'The only real mystery here is how your profession could be so easily taken for a ride.'

The sound of breaking glass prompted Marsh to stroll to the side of the house, where it seemed that Lord Swann had tried to unsuccessfully climb out of an antique window. His not inconsiderable bulk was now wedged half in and half out of the small, open window. He didn't look hurt but he did look truly pathetic.

'Have you ever heard of the *banality of evil,* Miss Lightfoot?' Marsh asked, pointing to the dangling figure of Lord Swann, 'Well, take a good look.'

16

There was a crash from the rear of The Lodge as Constable Gregory broke in through the back door. A moment later, he appeared at the front door and Inspector Marsh disappeared inside to haul Lord Swann back in through the bathroom window. Clover took that as her cue to return to Ellie and the children, who were finding the scene unfolding at The Lodge most interesting.

As Clover walked back over the lawn, a large, black Mercedes followed by a small, red Fiat pulled into the driveway. Sandy Delaney and Bettina Williams had arrived to collect the children. There were flurries of greeting as Jake, Josh and Olivia rushed over to hug their mums.

Jeremy Billingham came jogging out of the house to greet the parents with Mr Fish close behind him. 'Good morning and thank you so much for coming!' said Mr Billingham, as if he'd requested their help himself.

Bettina crouched down to chat in whispers with her boys but Sandy locked Mr Fish in her steely glare.

'Mr Fish, what exactly has been going on here?' she asked, ignoring Mr Billingham completely.

'Perhaps I can explain,' said Mr Billingham stepping between them. 'It's nothing at all really, merely an accidental injury to one of the education consultants who was attending an event on site.'

‘That hardly sounds like an appropriate reason to send the children home early,’ remarked Bettina Williams standing up to join the conversation.

‘We like to set the very highest standard for the experiences we offer the children,’ said Mr Billingham in a self-righteous tone. ‘It simply didn’t seem appropriate for them to stay. Though in truth there’s been no disruption to our visit at all.’

‘Mr Billingham, could I have a word with you please?’ asked Clover, keenly aware of the arrest that was taking place in the Lodge.

‘Not now, Miss Lightfoot,’ said Mr Billingham. ‘I’m very much in the middle of something here and I can assure you that my understanding of the situation is perfectly adequate. I suggest you spend more time engaging with the exceptional professional development opportunities that I’ve arranged for you this weekend and less time making mountains out of molehills.’

‘It’s just that...’ Clover began but she was cut off by a howl that came from the direction of the Lodge.

Lord Swann bolted out of the front door. He was not an athletic figure and his portly mass juddered and bounced as he ran with furious determination directly towards the Mercedes, perhaps hoping that the owner had left the keys inside. Barely a second passed before Constable Gregory appeared in hot pursuit of Lord Swann, who made it less than halfway across the lawn before Constable Gregory brought him down with a skilful lunge. The two of them tumbled over each other on the grass. Unused to any kind of physical activity, Lord Swann wheezed and squealed pathetically as Constable Gregory handcuffed him and helped him back to his feet.

Clover and Ellie immediately started to usher the children towards the cars, shutting them safely inside.

The terrible sounds issuing from Lord Swann brought the other consultants rushing out of the house to see what was going on. Zuzie ran towards her cousin while the others gathered on the steps outside of the house.

'Zuzie, tell them!' Lord Swann pleaded, 'I'd never do something like this, I'd never kill a man. I am a *businessman*! I freely admit that I acquired Neal's services to help me claw a little money back from those vampires at the insurance companies but you can't blame me for that can you? As for the rest of it, I was more surprised than anyone when it was so easy for Neal to convince you all that he really was an education consultant. The way I see it, that's your fault, not mine.'

'Why don't you tell them how much money you stood to make from a death on the premises?' said Inspector Marsh approaching unhurriedly, 'I'm afraid biting a police officer while resisting arrest does very little to convince me of your innocence,' he added, flexing his right hand that was wrapped in a handkerchief.

At this, Zuzie took a step back from Lord Swann, wrapping her arms around herself in horror, 'Oh William,' she said, 'how could you?' Hearing her words, Lord Swann seemed to finally admit defeat and he looked thoroughly ashamed of himself.

'I have more than enough evidence to make my case,' said Inspector Marsh. 'If you'll all remain on the premises for the next few hours, I'll see to it that everything is wrapped up by tonight.'

'Something isn't right,' said Clover quietly. All eyes turned towards her. She might have been self-conscious if she wasn't so lost in thought. 'What about the stolen manuscript?' she asked.

'It's my understanding that the manuscript was a worthless fake,' said Marsh dismissively.

'Yes, but whoever stole it didn't know that,' said Clover.

'I'm inclined to believe that all that might be unrelated to the murder,' said Marsh. 'Any one of the 'experts' might have decided to engage in a little illicit fact finding about a new rival in their field.'

'No, I don't think so,' said Clover. 'It's true that several of us went into Neal's room when we discovered that the door was open,' Clover glanced in Julie Giroux's direction, 'but I don't believe that anyone here would have broken the police seal on the door unless they had something extremely serious to hide.'

Inspector Marsh followed Clover's gaze towards to Julie Giroux, 'You're very astute, Miss Lightfoot, but I've followed up on that angle to my own satisfaction.'

Clover stood her ground. 'It doesn't add up,' she said, 'and I think I can prove it.'

17

Night fell quickly and the sun vanished behind the hills. The tower room was silent and Clover was alone in the gloom. The light from the downstairs landing threw a bright rectangle onto the corner of the ceiling but otherwise it left the room in almost complete darkness.

Now that the children had been safely taken home, the house was occupied only by the consultants and the teaching staff, most of them loitering rather listlessly in the dining hall, suitcases packed and ready to leave as soon as Inspector Marsh gave them permission. Marsh was examining documents in the small office room on the ground floor. It was obvious he wasn't taking Clover's conclusions seriously.

A soon as Clover had blurted out that she knew who the murderer was, she became painfully aware of how hard it would be to actually get the proof she needed. As far as Inspector Marsh was concerned, Lord Swann was the prime suspect and there was no reason to look for anyone else. He had a suspect with a motive and the opportunity to carry out the crime. That was all there was to it. She wasn't about to give up now but Clover felt very apprehensive. She'd been sitting alone on her bed for almost an hour, her heart was racing and she was alert to the slightest sound.

When Clover did see a movement there was no noise just a change in the light shining up the stairs. Someone was making their way up to her room and they were doing it very stealthily and carefully.

'Come up, you don't need to stay quiet, I've seen you now,' said Clover. Wooden floorboards creaked in response and a figure emerged in the doorway.

It was Gryff.

'I know what you did,' said Clover trying to keep her voice steady.

'What do you mean, Miss Lightfoot? I don't know what you're talking about. I just came to see how you are, that's all. You should really be careful, though, declaring that there's a murderer on the premises and then running off to hide up here on your own. It seems rather unwise, don't you think?'

'Everything pointed to it being you, trying to threaten me only confirms it.'

'Threats...' said Gryff. 'Hypothetically speaking, if I'd killed Neal then I probably wouldn't need to threaten anyone at this point. Lord Swann is the prime suspect and he's up to his ears in the lies he has told, everything points to him being guilty. If I actually had killed Neal then it would practically be the perfect crime. But I'm talking hypothetically of course. Even if I could get away with something like this, why would I bother? There's no obvious motive.'

'Oh, I think there is,' said Clover. 'You were clearly jealous of Neal and you were intimidated by his growing popularity.'

'Me?' Gryff laughed. 'Intimidated by Neal's fame? I'm a household name, Neal was a nobody.'

‘I don’t know about that. You saw that Neal had got Julie Giroux’s attention and if you happened to find out that Julie had a contract with Neal to publish his ideas then I’m sure that would have been even more galling. It’s no wonder you were so envious of him.’

The dark silhouette of Gryff’s cheek twitched as he took a step closer to Clover, ‘I assure you, I had nothing whatsoever to be jealous about. Neal was a fraud. I could see that from the start, even if everyone else was slow to realise it.’

‘But he was such a successful fraud,’ said Clover. ‘It looked as if he actually might make a name for himself as an educational consultant with nothing more than a forged identity and some made-up activities. My guess is that you asked Neal for a private meeting to see if you could bully him into sharing some of his ideas with you.’

‘I didn’t meet with Neal. I have an alibi, I was with Sophie King that night.’

‘She’s so in love with you that she regularly lies about your relationship. That’s no alibi at all.’

‘Even if that’s true, Miss Lightfoot, it doesn’t mean I had anything to do with Neal’s death.’

‘I think it does,’ said Clover. ‘When you were demonstrating your ideas about *The Hero’s Journey*, you revealed to us exactly how you think. You wanted to keep your position as a celebrity teaching consultant more than anything in the world and you saw Neal as the monster you had to kill to get what you wanted.’

Gryff didn’t deny her accusation this time but took another step closer to Clover, moving completely into the shadows.

‘Neal was a liar and a fool,’ he said. ‘Whatever happened to him, he deserved it. You’re a teacher, you must be able to understand that. Neal’s manuscript contained nothing more than empty rituals and vague superstitions wrapped up in pseudo-science to make them sound more plausible. It was a monstrous distortion of the truth. It’s better that Neal’s lies died with him.’

‘How could you know about the rest of Neal’s ideas unless you saw his manuscript? You broke into Neal’s room and took his work, didn’t you?’

‘So what if I did? Maybe I was curious, it doesn’t mean I killed him.’

‘But you did, didn’t you?’ said Clover backing away from him.

‘Of course I did,’ Gryff had lowered his voice to a dangerous whisper. ‘If something as blatantly silly as *Mind-Robics* had become popular, then sooner or later our profession would end up as a laughing stock.’

‘I can see how that would be a particular problem for you,’ said Clover. ‘Perhaps it would also cause people to take a more critical look at your own work. I don’t see that your ideas are any more substantiated than Neal’s. His success didn’t just make you jealous, it threatened your livelihood too.’

Gryff took two quick steps forward and Clover stumbled back against the windowsill. ‘Listen to me, Miss Lightfoot. Neal wanted to be the hero of his own story but, in the end, he wasn’t prepared to do what was necessary to accomplish that, whereas I am always prepared to do *whatever* is required, however messy it might become.’

Gryff leaned in closer and now there was nowhere for Clover to go. ‘Miss Lightfoot,’ he said, ‘if you ever want to see the sunshine again then I want to hear you promise that you’re going to keep your suspicions to yourself. Otherwise, well, a fall from this height would surely be fatal.’

‘You won’t get away with this,’ said Clover, ‘everyone’s going to know what you’re really like, Jacqui Scarfe was right to call you a parasite but you’re even more dangerous than that, you’re a predator.’ Her voice trembled as Gryff towered over her and she flinched as he placed his hand on the window frame, boxing her in. ‘I’m going to expose you,’ she said, defiantly.

‘How exactly are you going to do that?’ asked Gryff as he started to slide the window open.

‘You’re the expert in *The Hero’s Journey,*’ replied Clover. ‘In their darkest hour the hero is given a *magical weapon*. Something the monster never sees coming, isn’t that what you said?’

Gryff hesitated as the cool night air washed in from the darkness outside. For a moment he was puzzled, then Clover snapped her fingers.

Suddenly, a furious blaze of white light flooded the room from outside the dark window. It seemed as if the sun had risen again in the sky. Gryff was completely dazzled. ‘What is it?’ he gasped into the searing light, trying to shield his eyes with his hands.

For one satisfying moment, Clover wondered whether Gryff was imagining that the spirits of Hatton Hoo had come to claim him or perhaps he was thinking that the ghost of Neal Skinner had come to speak the truth from beyond the grave.

Her thoughts were interrupted by the tweet of a tiny electronic fanfare.

‘Why does it make those silly sounds?’ someone asked, looking towards the light.

Tom poked his head in through the window. ‘It’s quite an expensive video camera,’ he said, much better than the one we have at school but it seems to make all kinds of funny little noises whenever you change the setting on it.’ Tom was kneeling on the fire escape outside the window with the video camera pointed into the room. ‘I switched off the *night vision* setting when I turned the spotlight on and that set off the fanfare.’

Gryff squinted into the light and the colour drained from his face as he noticed the microphone mounted on a stand beside him on the bedside table. A thin cable ran outside and it was plugged into the camera. Tom had been recording everything.

‘You can’t show that to anyone,’ Gryff spluttered.

'Oh but I'm afraid that we already have,' said Clover. 'Tom's very good at setting up this sort of thing and Lord Swann seems to have invested in a good deal of equipment. That cable there,' she pointed at the back of the camera, 'leads all the way downstairs to the TV in the classroom. As soon as we started talking, Ellie went to find inspector Marsh and show him what was happening. I imagine he's on his way up here now that the show's almost over.'

'I think she was planning to ask the other consultants to watch as well,' said Tom. 'It would be a shame if they missed out.'

'No!' protested Gryff but all the strength had gone from his voice. 'So you planned all this to trap me?'

'Mr Parr, in my job I have to plan the best way of teaching people a lesson, then I carry those plans out, all day, every day. I'd like to think that I have developed some skills in that direction.'

Gryff's horror and fury were evident but there was nothing he could do as he heard boots thudding up the stairs. 'But how did you do this? You're just a teacher,' he muttered.

'You really need to spend more time with the people you're supposed to be advising,' said Clover. I don't think there's a single one of us who is *just* a teacher. Underestimate us at your peril.' She turned her back on him and shared a smile with Tom as Inspector Marsh put his hand on Gryff's shoulder.

'Time to go home, at last,' said Clover. 'I think I learned a lot this weekend after all.'

Epilogue

Easter 1997

Gryff was running desperately through the street holding a raincoat pulled completely over his head. He glanced out from under the flapping collar and the TV image of him froze capturing a portrait of him giving a vindictive glare.

A newsreader's voice spoke over the still image, 'The trial of Gryffin Parr concluded today as his appeal collapsed and Mr Parr was taken down to begin his sentence.'

The scene shifted to a surly looking Inspector Marsh, 'It was an unusual case but I'm very glad that justice was done,' said Marsh to the reporter.

'Inspector Marsh, what do you say to the rumours about the case being solved by a primary school teacher?' a reporter asked.

'We're always grateful for the help and cooperation of members of the public when it comes to bringing criminals to justice but I don't have anything to add to my previous comments,' replied Marsh with a grimace.

The doorbell rang and Clover hastily turned off the TV. It was Tom. He looked quite shy standing on her doorstep. It was the first time he'd ever visited her flat and she let him inside with a broad smile.

'Go on through to the kitchen,' Clover said, 'I'm in the middle of a little culinary experiment I'd like to try out on you.'

'I brought this,' said Tom, fishing a bottle of wine out of his rucksack, 'I hope that's not inappropriate of me.'

Clover laughed, 'No, of course not. Of all people, I can safely say, you've never done anything even slightly inappropriate,' she turned away to check the oven.

Clover's kitchen was tiny and Tom hovered by the fridge, suddenly seeming unsure of what to say next.

He removed a pony-shaped magnet from a leaflet on Clover's fridge door and read out the title: '*Swann Hall: Hatton Hoo Visitors' Centre and Pony Sanctuary.*' He looked at her inquiringly.

'Oh yes, that was Zuzie Zuleika's doing,' said Clover. 'It seems she's quite the organiser. She's created a trust to develop the new visitors centre for Hatton Hoo and with the money from that she's managed to buy Swann Hall herself.'

Tom looked at the other items stuck to the fridge and his eyes alighted on a typed letter with the words *Buckington University* printed at the top. 'Is this the famous letter?' Tom asked.

'It is,' said Clover, 'and I'm very flattered. I kept in touch with Bernard purely out of interest in his research. I never imagined he'd make me a job offer.'

'I think you'd be amazing in teacher training,' said Tom. 'I've learned so much from watching you work. Do you think you'll take it?'

Clover sighed, 'I'm not sure. Ellie wants to take a year out and go travelling. I've been thinking about going with her.'

'That's sounds really exciting, where would you go?'

'Oh, all over I expect, a year's a long time. If I'm ever going to do it, this is my opportunity. I haven't really got any reason to stay here,' she carefully avoided looking at him and concentrated on opening the wine.

'You could always jump into Mr Billingham's shoes,' said Tom. 'I didn't think he'd move on so quickly. I suppose he wasn't really cut out to be a Deputy Head.'

'I think he did the right thing, he's obviously an entrepreneur at heart,' said Clover. 'I'm happy for him, it seems like he finally decided what he really wants.' She took a sip of wine and tried to catch Tom's eye but he continued to study the bits and pieces stuck to the fridge. Clover shook her head, how could she be so bad at getting through to him?

'I have some news actually,' said Tom without looking up. 'I'm planning on leaving the school at the end of this year. It turns out that my computer skills might come in pretty handy in the outside world. A few friends and I are going to start an internet website.'

'That's interesting,' said Clover, surprised. 'I've heard of people doing that...' She suddenly didn't know what to say.

'I've always thought...' Tom hesitated. 'I didn't think it would be very professional to have a relationship with someone I worked with.'

Clover looked around at him, 'Really?' she asked, surprised.

'Well...yes,' said Tom, blushing.

'Ha!' said Clover, 'I just thought I was terrible at flirting.'

'No, not at all, Miss Lightfoot,' said Tom. 'In fact, I'd have to say, I find you entirely exceptional at everything, flirting included...'

Clover Lightfoot will return

Investigate at

www.goodreads.com/CloverLightfoot

Also available:

A School Inspector Calls

or

“OfsDead!”

Miss Clover Lightfoot Murder Mystery No. 1

Made in the USA
Middletown, DE
31 May 2017